HE WAS A FARMER.

SHE WAS A LADY.

WERE THEY TO FALL IN LOVE,

NOTHING COULD COME OF IT . . .

OR COULD IT?

HIGH GARTH

by Mira Stables

FAWCETT COVENTRY ● NEW YORK

HIGH GARTH

THIS BOOK CONTAINS THE COMPLETE TEXT OF
THE ORIGINAL HARDCOVER EDITION.

Published by Fawcett Coventry Books, a unit of CBS Publications, the Consumer Publishing Division of CBS Inc., by arrangement with Robert Hale Limited.

ISBN: 0-449-50032-2

Printed in the United States of America

First Fawcett Coventry printing: April 1980

10 9 8 7 6 5 4 3 2 1

For all my friends in the Dales
who have encouraged me,
by claiming to enjoy my stories,
and
especially for Nell
who walked the green tracks with me.

Author's Note

Those who know the Yorkshire Dales will find themselves on familiar ground. The place has not changed so much in a hundred and fifty years. But High Garth and the people who lived there, and the sink hole known as the Gullet, exist only in the author's imagination.

M.S.

ONE

March had come in like a lion, but the private parlour at the Pheasant was surprisingly comfortable for so small a posting inn. With a good fire blazing in the hearth and a high-backed settle drawn up to it to protect the traveller from any wandering draught, it was positively cosy, even without the added emphasis of the blustering gale that was rattling the casements and hurling an occasional flurry of hail and sleet against the window panes.

But the gentleman who was prowling up and down its well-polished floor seemed unappreciative of his good fortune. His brows were knit in a heavy frown. From time to time he pulled out an old fashioned time-piece from the inner pocket of his well-worn coat, and since this faithful servant refused to lie to him, his annoyance became more obvious on each occasion; though perhaps it was the firelight, striking red gleams from tawny hair worn slightly too long to be fashionable, and the scarce-controlled energy in the long supple stride that gave the impression of feral anger.

A log falling apart drew him to the comfort of the hearth. He kicked the blazing embers back with a shabby boot and drew a slim packet of letters from his pocket. There were three of them, but after a cursory glance he dropped two into the heart of the fire. The third he re-read with more care, put it back in his pocket, and resumed his restless pacing.

The sound of footsteps approaching the parlour door caused him to glance up with a certain lightening of expression, but when it was only the landlady who came in, the frown returned.

"Still no one?" he queried abruptly.

"A letter, sir," said Mrs. Robertson, proffering it. "The guard from the stage walked across from the Feathers with it. Said the lady had left the coach at Leyburn but had given him a shilling to deliver her letter."

In deference to the landlady, Mr. Delvercourt swallowed an oath and mentally consigned all shilly-shallying females to the devil. The terms of his advertisement had been perfectly plain, yet the two applicants whom he had already interviewed had been hopelessly unsuitable, while the third—the most promising of the three—had obviously changed her mind. He would have to advertise again. *More* delay—and possibly another day devoted to interviewing prospective housekeepers—when, with lambing already begun, he was urgently needed elsewhere.

Mrs. Robertson was still waiting. He turned to nod dismissal. She said diffidently, "Will you be requiring the parlour any longer, sir? Not that it's likely we'll have more guests in this sort of weather, but I'd not like to be sending any one up here if your honour was still wanting to be private."

8

Mr. Delvercourt's features relaxed into a smile so attractive that it was easy to see why the good lady accorded such deference to one who bore all the appearance of a hard-working and impoverished farmer.

"No, indeed, Mrs. Robertson. If I may ask ten minutes more grace? I must read this pesky female's letter, and then, I fear, draft another advertisement. It will save time if I do it now. Then I shall look forward to one of your suppers—and my bed. For I must set out betimes tomorrow." He considered the attractive prospect of a bowl of rum punch to follow the supper, decided that it was unwarrantable extravagance, and sat down at the writing table.

The letter was much as he had anticipated. The lady had decided that High Garth was too isolated and had accepted another post. He shrugged, crumpled up the missive, tossed it into the hearth and set himself to composition. It was not easy. High Garth was indeed remote, the wage that he could offer was small. And the existence of Philip complicated the business. A competent housekeeper might have been found fairly easily—some decent widow, perhaps. But one who would also undertake the charge of a lively six-year-old, check his capacity for getting into mischief—and danger—and supervise his first lessons, was a far more difficult proposition. He thought of the two candidates whom he had already rejected, the one a genteel spinster of uncertain age, utterly out of place in a farm kitchen and probably ineffectual as a governess, the other a sturdy wench, plump, comely and capable-seeming, but with an acquisitive gleam in her eye and a frank assessment of his own person that had given plain warning of her intentions. A man who needed a housekeeper was presumably fair game, but that young woman had been a little *too* obvious. He grinned wry-

9

ly. She would have found poor pickings at High Garth and scant compensation in *his* charms. He doubted if her plans for making the post a permanent one would have outlasted the first week.

It seemed that his needs demanded a non-pareil. He sighed, added another five pounds to the salary that he could so ill afford, and put the pen aside. The money would have to be found somehow. Janet was aging, and despite her fierce protestations the work was too much for her. While the thought of Philip running wild all summer with no one to keep him from the dangers that awaited the heedless adventurer in that harsh countryside, was more than he could sustain. Last summer had been difficult enough. He could have filled every minute twice over with urgent tasks, and the five-year-old Philip, timid and inclined to tears in the insecurity of a new way of life, had clung to him closer than a shadow. Very much in the way he had been at times, but at least Patrick had known where he was. But a year had wrought a vast change. Philip had settled down almost *too* well; had come to realize the delightful possibilities of the new regime. No longer was there Nurse, a couple of nursery maids, and any number of other interfering adults to fuss over him and scold over most of his activities. There was not even that rather frightening bearded gentleman known as Papa, whom Philip had decided was God's brother. Both, to Philip, meant an unnatural state of cleanliness and an insistence that he stay still and quiet under uncomfortable conditions. God lived in the church, where you were shut up in a kind of a box called a pew and couldn't see anything interesting. But you only had to go and visit him on Sundays. Papa lived in the library. The seats were more comfortable than God's, though a small boy's feet still didn't reach the floor, and there were nice things to look at. But you had to visit Papa every night, and Papa, unlike God, had a way of booming out sudden questions to which Philip rarely knew the answers. Then he would hang his head, knowing that Papa was disappointed or angry by the way his beard waggled.

When first he had come to live with Patrick at High Garth, he had been surprised but pleased to discover that neither God nor Papa had further need of his attendance. Papa, explained Patrick, had gone to stay with God. Philip could understand *that* Had not he himself come to stay with Patrick? They were only half brothers, and Patrick was quite grown up, but he was a very good sort of brother to have. He knew a lot of interesting things, even if his hand was much harder than Nurse's had been. As for going to church every Sunday, Patrick said it was too far to walk and that Maggy had worked all week and deserved her rest. Philip was well content. Janet heard him say his prayers every night, but he could gabble those off without really thinking. And there was so much to see and to do and to ask about on the farm that he didn't really miss the Court, except for his pony. And Patrick had promised that he should have another pony, if he could buy one reasonably at the horse fair. Meanwhile there were lambs and calves and chickens. He was allowed to feed them. And not even Janet grumbled about grubby hands and muddy boots, though she *did* scold when he tore his smalls, and asked him if he thought they grew on trees, a remark that Philip thought exquisitely funny.

During the long winter, trying to cope with a small boy's energy in the intervals between feeding stock and dealing with all the maintenance jobs that must be done on a farm when other work is at a standstill,

Patrick had looked ahead to the busy days of spring and summer and had realized that something must be done about Philip. There were not even any other children for him to play with. And he was too young to be sent to school. A governess—firm without being too strict, and energetic, too—was the obvious answer. But he also wanted to relieve Janet of the arduous task of housekeeping, so willingly undertaken for love of himself, and he simply could not afford two wages, two more mouths to be fed. It was make and scrape as it was, and every spare penny to be saved for Philip's schooling when the time came.

He sighed. And absentmindedly succumbed to the invitation of the high-backed settle, stretching out long legs to the comfort of the fire and resting his head against the solid red cushion that had been hung at just the right height to give its support. He had been at work before dawn to win himself time for this fruitless journey, and now it would be all to do again. His lids drooped. Within five minutes he was deeply asleep.

He woke to the sound of voices. "You'll be all right here, miss. Very respectable house, the Pheasant, and Mrs. Robertson a kindly soul. Now there's your ticket for the stage. Nine o'clock tomorrow from the Feathers yard, but it's only a step down the road." The voice, immediately identifiable to a discerning ear as that of a man-servant, middle-aged and responsible, took on a note of resentment. "Might have bought you a seat in the Mail. You'll be shaken to bits in the stage, let alone taking two days longer! Well—talking pays no toll—so I'll bid you good evening, miss, and Mrs. Porter and me hopes you'll find a good post as soon as maybe. We'll both of us miss you sore, and that's a fact."

12

"And I shall miss you, so good as you've both been to me." The answering voice was clear and pleasant. "I'll write to Mrs. Porter as soon as I'm settled in a new post. And will you give her this. No," as inarticulate noises of protest were heard, "it is only a handkerchief that I have been embroidering, but it will serve to remind her of the girl she so kindly mothered."

"She'll treasure it dearly, miss, I know she will." The voice was gruff with feeling. "And we both of us think it a right shame to turn you off so. It wasn't your blame."

Never mind, John. At least I wasn't turned off without a character!" There was a hint of a smile in the girl's voice.

"So I should think, miss. The least they could do, after the way you've managed those young rapscallions. But I'd best be off, 'fore someone starts enquiring why I've been so long. And you'll be sure and write to the missus?"

"Indeed I will. And who knows? Perhaps some day we'll meet again."

The parlour door closed. Still a little dazed by the mists of sleep and guiltily aware of having listened to a private conversation not intended for his ears, Mr. Delvercourt caught a sound suspiciously like a sob. It brought him erect as one stung, clearing his throat with quite unnecessary energy to draw attention to his presence and making pretence of rubbing sleep-bleared eyes and stifling a yawn as he said, "So sorry, ma'am. Must have dropped off. Thought myself alone. Didn't imagine anyone else'd be abroad on such a dirty night."

Another blast of hail obligingly rattled the casement to add point to this remark. "Shocking, ain't it?" he drawled, deliberately rustic, and crossed to the window to allow the girl time to recover herself.

It *had* been a sob. But the handkerchief had been whisked out of sight at his first words and he saw the instinctive bracing of slim shoulders as she swung round to face him.

"I beg your pardon, sir," she said stiffly. "I was assured that I would be private in the parlour."

"So you should be, ma'am," he apologized. "I told Mrs. Robertson I'd go down to the coffee room as soon as I'd drafted my advertisement—and then fell asleep instead. I'll take myself off at once." He hesitated briefly, then succumbed to the gambling instinct that in one form or another had been for centuries a Delvercourt characteristic. "Just for a moment I thought you might be another young lady come to apply for the post. But of course you're not. Pray forgive me." He bowed slightly and moved towards the door.

He was well pleased when, even as he lifted the latch, the girl said slowly, "A post, sir? What kind of post? It so chances that I am, in fact, seeking a new situation, but I have not yet applied for one and am not come in answer to your advertisement."

He turned towards her but made no move to return to the hearth. "Not an easy post to fill," he said ruefully, "as I have been discovering all afternoon. And not, I fear, a suitable one for a young lady who looks and speaks as you do."

She studied him curiously. She knew very well that it was unwise, even potentially dangerous, to fall into conversation with a casual stranger. But surely nothing could happen to her in a respectable inn. She was depressed and anxious. Her future was uncertain and far from bright. There could be no harm in talking for a little while. The gentleman did not seem to be of an

14

encroaching disposition—indeed he was plainly poised on the edge of departure. It might be that listening to the recital of *his* difficulties would help her, briefly, to forget her own.

Being herself of a forthright disposition, she said lightly, "Where, then, do you place me in the social scale? And what is the position for which my speech and my appearance render me ineligible?"

Cool hazel eyes scanned her thoughtfully. Yet the frank appraisal was not offensive—and she *had* asked him. She sustained it with composure.

"I place you as a gently-bred, well-educated female of independent mind, a little past her first youth," he told her coolly. "I would suspect that you earn your bread as a companion or a governess—probably the latter, since you are rather young for the other post."

It was extremely reprehensible, but Miss Ann Beverley badly wanted to laugh. Fortunately the remark about her age rankled sufficiently to enable her to keep her countenance. She curtsied slightly. "You are percipient, sir. And I am four and twenty. Pray tell me more of the paragon *you* seek."

"I fear she has no existence outside my hopeful dreams," he said, shaking his head regretfully but matching her own light tone. "My housekeeper, though quite indomitable, is too frail for the perpetual drudgery of a primitive farmhouse. But whoever undertakes to relieve her of the heavier work must also manage to persuade her that she is still quite indispensable and submit patiently to her occasional crotchets. Just in case this is not asking enough, there is also my small brother who stands in sore need of companionship, correction and instruction, not to mention the whole time services of a guardian angel with sufficient foresight to outpace his ingenious

15

brain. Show me a woman willing to undertake such a labour and I will tell you that her price is above rubies. Or, to descend from the poetic to the practical, that she should command a handsome salary and be given every possible comfort and assistance with her formidable task. I, on the other hand, can offer a beggarly twenty five pounds a year, the help of two young maids, willing enough but wholly untrained, and no modern comforts whatsoever. Do you wonder that I doubt the possibility of the lady's existence?"

Ann Beverly was staring at him in growing astonishment. During the past five years she had held a number of posts and had been interviewed by many different types of employer, but this was the first time that she had heard anyone express concern for the difficulties which the applicant might encounter. These were always minimized. Spoiled children were described as 'so high spirited'; selfish, tyrannical females who enjoyed ill-health simply for lack of better distraction, became 'martyrs to migraine'—or whatever complaint they had elected—'so brave, so patient'. One was expected to feel that it was a privilege to serve these rare spirits in return for the merest pittance. To hear someone openly proclaim that the post he was offering was no sinecure certainly compelled the attention. It even invited further investigation.

"And a well-educated young woman, no longer in her first youth, is not suited to such a position?" she enquired mischievously—indeed rather rashly on such brief acquaintance.

He had the grace to look slightly ashamed. "I should apologize for my extremely personal remarks, ma'am," he said stiffly. "Ruralizing has done nothing for my manners. As for suitability—you may well be an excellent governess. You will forgive me if I beg leave to

16

question your domestic capabilities. You have not exactly the appearance of one accustomed to manage economically for a hungry household in humble circumstances."

That was a compliment worth having, thought Ann, well-pleased, because it was quite unwitting. He was not to know that her scrupulously neat travelling dress owed its fashionable appearance to her own clever fingers. She said cheerfully, "Now there, sir, you are sadly mistaken. I may have had the advantage of a good education, but I fear I am *not* a very successful governess. My domestic capabilities, on the other hand, are of a very high order. Upon leaving school I was obliged for some time to keep house for my stepfather. His notions of holding household were nipcheese if not downright miserly. I learned to market, to wash and mend, brew and bake, to preserve fruit and game in season—oh—all the attributes that go to the making of a good housekeeper, with every farthing accounted for and not so much as a crust wasted. Which just shows that you should never judge by appearances, doesn't it? Still—I wish you well in your search, and I hope you find your paragon."

The pleasant words were plainly dismissive. Mr. Delvercourt was aware of a distinct desire to prolong the encounter, a desire which Fate chose to favour, for at that moment Mrs. Robertson came in.

The landlady was slightly flustered and apologetic. "I reckoned you was gone down to the coffee room, sir," she began breathlessly. "I'm sure I'm ever so sorry, miss. I quite thought the parlour was empty. 'Twasn't till I took Mr. Delvercourt's supper in that I found he was still up here. Don't let it spoil, will you, sir? One of my meat puddings, and the pastry light as a feather. Now miss, how about you? Will you take a

17

bit o' supper in the coffee room or shall I carry a tray to your bedchamber?" She saw the girl hesitate and added encouragingly, "There's a bonny fire in the coffee room. And no need to be shy of Mr. Delvercourt here. I've known him this many a year and you can take my word for it he's none of your fly-by-nights but a respectable hard-working farmer."

Both her guests laughed. The girl said diffidently, "I own it to be a strong temptation. A fire, hot food, *and* respectable company." And that will teach him to make remarks about people's ages, she decided, little guessing how accurately her expression reflected her thoughts.

"*And* saves work for me," nodded Mrs. Robertson briskly, as though that settled it. "I'll show you your room, miss. You'll be wanting to take that damp cloak off. And do you, sir, go down right away and set to, for letting good victuals go cold for manners' sake is what I don't hold with."

She swept her guests to their respective destinations without hindrance, though the gentleman paid no further heed to her advice, choosing rather to let his supper cool, and forgetting economy so far as to order a bottle of wine. The chance encounter had amused him. He was not likely to set eyes on the girl again. There could be no harm in beguiling away a dull evening in pleasant converse.

18

TWO

"But I think you've run mad!" exclaimed Miss Barbara Beverly, her eyes dark with dismay. "A man you know nothing about, save that he is advertising a post that is next door to slavery in a place that is so savage and isolated that anything could happen to you and it might well be months before we heard of it. Oh! Very well, then. So you saw the original advertisement. So the landlady—and how should she know—said he was respectable. It doesn't alter the fact that the work is menial. You know perfectly well that Miss Vestey would let you stay here, helping with the little ones, until I am married. Jack is due home in the summer and we are planning the wedding for September. Then you may come and live with us. And spend a few months 'wholly devoted to pleasure' as Papa Fortune would say. And I'm sure no one has ever deserved it more," she ended heartily, for the sisters loved each other dearly, despite their differences. Each admired

—or deplored—facets in the other's personality that were lacking in her own, but during a happy childhood, gypsying about Europe with their soldier father, and even more determinedly during a difficult girlhood, when their widowed mama had re-married, they had developed a family solidarity that admitted criticism only between themselves.

"I imagine Jack will have something to say about that," suggested Ann mildly. "To be taking your wife's twin sister on your honeymoon would scarcely be to most men's taste, even if there *is* no danger of mistaking which is which." For Barbara was petite and brunette, while she, save for the dark eyes which both had inherited from their mother, was silver fair, like Papa, and built, as she ruefully complained, on Amazonian lines. In which she did herself less than justice, for although she was admittedly tall for a woman, she was slight of build and moved with a lithe grace that was wholly feminine.

"Goose," laughed Barbara. "You know I didn't mean on the honeymoon—though Jack has promised to take me to Spain and to Portugal, and it would have been fun to re-visit some of our childhood haunts under peaceful conditions, wouldn't it? No. But when we come home, you will join us at Mickleford and we'll indulge all the extravagant whims that Papa Fortune so firmly suppressed. Can you not be patient till then, and stay quietly here instead of stravaiging off to the wilds of Yorkshire on some madcap ploy?"

If Barbara thought that her sister meant to hang on Jack Broughton's sleeve, she was out in her reckoning. Ann did not deny that it would be very comfortable to have a secure refuge, a place where one could always be sure of a welcome if matters were desperate, but she had no intention of taking up permanent residence at Mickleford Hall, nor even of making any prolonged stay there. Perhaps later, when the babies came along, she might be of use to her sister. That would be a different pair of shoes. Meanwhile she meant to cling to her independence. But there was no point in provoking an argument on that head.

"Have a little pity on poor Miss Vestey," she teased. "If she had to suffer me for the better part of a twelve-month, *she* would certainly explode even if I didn't. I'm sure she was never so thankful to see the back of a departing pupil as on the day that I left. As for helping with the little ones, I should detest it of all things, since I am perfectly well aware that it is only offered to please you! Now don't take that in snuff. Of *course* the future Lady Broughton is a patron to be studied! Do you really believe that if you were just an ordinary governess you would be allotted such a comfortable room? Why—there is even space to set up a trucklebed when your wilful sister descends upon you, which she does, alas, all too often! If it were not for your prospects of future grandeur, you'd be fortunate to have a *bed* to yourself, let alone a whole room. And remember that *I* certainly couldn't expect such favourable treatment. No, my love. Not for worlds would I miss your wedding, and I'll be very happy to visit you when you're wed and to hear all about your travels, but you must know I couldn't possibly stay cooped up here."

Barbara did know it. Ann's energy, her zest for adventure and for a wider world to conquer, had always been something to acknowledge, even if one did not understand them. She got up, shook out her skirts, and said calmly, "I must go. It's my turn to take the older girls for their walk. We'll talk further tonight," and went contentedly enough about her prescribed duties.

Left to herself, Ann went over to the window-seat and stared out unseeingly at the prospect of a bare-looking kitchen garden. She was very tired, for she had not arrived until noon and John Porter's predictions about the discomforts of the stage had been amply fulfilled. In her present state of aching fatigue that odd encounter at the Pheasant seemed dream-like. Had she really sat at supper with a stranger, accepted a glass of wine from him, told him how she had come to be dismissed from her post and provisionally accepted the one that he offered? At least, she reflected, she had clung to *some* vestige of common-sense, since she had refused to commit herself finally without knowing a little more about him.

"You will expect *me* to furnish references," she had pointed out. "I think I am entitled to some reassurance as to *your* standing in the community. The vicar of your parish, perhaps?"

He had laughed at that. "Actually I am not in the least interested in your references," he had told her. "They could scarcely apply in this situation and in any case I prefer to form my own judgements. But I do see that your position is rather different. Unfortunately the vicar of my present parish would not know me if he saw me. Since High Garth is several miles from his church I fear I am become little better than a heathen. There is my attorney—but no. You might think him to be in collusion with me. Will nothing but a clergyman serve?"

His eyes were smiling, making her feel that her scruples were faintly ridiculous, but she clung to them the more obstinately for that. Eventually he hit upon the notion of writing to the rector of the parish in which he had resided before removing to High Garth. "I believe he will give me a good character," he had submitted meekly, amusement still dancing in the hazel eyes, "and I shall beg him to write to you at once, so that I may look forward to your arrival at High Garth on the first of next month."

It was only next day, jolting along in the stage, a trifle disappointed that she had not seen her prospective employer again, he having left an hour and more before she came down to breakfast, that she remembered. The first of next month was All Fools' Day. Had he meant to drop her a hint that he had just been amusing himself? Whiling away the hours of a dull evening? Would the letter ever come? He had seemed serious enough when he warned her of the difficulties in store, meticulous in ascertaining the details of Barbara's address. In the peaceful seclusion of her sister's room she pondered these questions for the hundredth time; then decided that she was too weary to be capable of fair judgement. She took off her dress and shoes and lay down on the bed, pulled the quilt over her and fell instantly and deeply asleep.

It was dusk when Barbara's return wakened her. She was much refreshed by her long sleep, and by the time that she had washed her hands and face and rebraided her hair was inclined to take a more cheerful view of her future. "What a relief not to have to put on a cap," she commented, studying the scrupulously neat coronal in a somewhat inadequate mirror. "I shall have to make some new ones, though, to take to Yorkshire. It will be something to fill the waiting time. And there is nothing that lends one such an air of sobriety and responsibility as a well starched cap." Barbara, hurriedly changing her own dress for supper,

23

declined the provocative challenge. If Ann's heart was set on going, go she would.

If anything had been needed to confirm Ann in her choice, the supper hour supplied it. The dull, if sufficient, fare, the long lines of meek girlish faces bent decorously over their plates, the occasional murmurs of subdued conversation, these were not for her. She wondered how Barbara had endured it for so long. But of course Barbara had Jack and a secure and happy future to dream about. Lacking that solace, surely even she must have rebelled. Private governessing might have its hazards, but really!

She was drawn into discussion of those hazards later that night when they were at last permitted to retire after an insipid evening in Miss Vestey's prim parlour discussing such absorbing topics as the present circumstances of several former school-mates whom the sisters might recall, and the recent shocking increase in the prices of various staple commodities. Fortunately good manners prevented Miss Vestey from asking outright why her former pupil had left the Anstruthers, but no such inhibition curbed her twin's curiosity.

Barbara waited only until the bedroom door was safe shut behind them before demanding, "Now. Let's have it. How *did* you come to resign a post that, when last you wrote to me, sounded eminently desirable? If I remember aright, you liked both Mr. and Mrs. Anstruther and your only complaint was that their mother indulged the children beyond what was reasonable, which made them difficult to manage. Yes! And you said that even the servants treated you with proper respect, which is rare indeed. So what went wrong?"

"I didn't resign," said her sister mischievously. "I was turned off. But not without a character," she offered demurely, seeing Barbara's shocked face.

"But what did you *do*?" demanded that outraged damsel. "They couldn't just turn you out like that! You must have done something *dreadful*."

"They could and they did. And as for doing something dreadful, you'd have done exactly the same yourself. Well, no, you couldn't, of course, not being tall enough, but you'd have *wanted* to."

"*Will* you tell a plain tale!" exclaimed her exasperated twin.

"I only boxed Mr. Luxton's ears," protested Ann virtuously. "He is Mrs. Anstruther's cousin, and a revolting little beast—one of the patting squeezing kind —and seemed to think that I should be flattered by his odious attentions."

"But they surely didn't dismiss you for that? They can't have wanted you to encourage him and must have realized that he deserved it."

"Well Mr. Delvercourt certainly said it served him right. But there *is* a little more to it than that." She stopped, looking guilty but smug.

Barbara sighed resignedly. "I might have guessed as much. Go on!"

"It all comes of being so tall," explained the defendant. "If I were tiny, like you, I couldn't have stretched up to put my bedroom candlestick on the shelf where they were kept during the day. But I did. And that was when Mr. Luxton chose to come creeping up behind me and begin his horrid mauling, putting his arms round me and fondling my bosom. Wouldn't *you* have boxed his ears?"

"Yes. But I still don't see"—

"Only that in my surprise and alarm I had—I had— er— *neglected* to put down the candlestick. And it was a heavy brass one." She peeped at Barbara, trying not to laugh.

"Heavens! Did you kill him?"

"Of course I didn't—else I'd be in jail, silly. He dodged back, so that I caught his face rather than the side of his head. The doctor said that his nose was broken and he had lost two teeth. He was certainly a horrid sight, but he will live to pester some other helpless female."

"Not so helpless!" murmured Barbara.

"That is exactly what Mr. Delvercourt said. Also that he could see that they had no choice but to dismiss me. I had, he explained very kindly, struck at the root of the whole social system with my candlestick, and went on-to paint a most moving picture of the Anstruthers unable to sleep nights for fear of me plotting revolution in my garret—for so he chose to describe my perfectly comfortable bedchamber. But since he also described Mr. Luxton as a slimy toad, I found myself perfectly in charity with him and was able to sustain his frivolous comments with fortitude."

Barbara laughed, a little uneasily. There was considerable doubt in face and voice as she said slowly, "He sounds a very odd kind of farmer."

Ann hesitated only briefly. They had never had secrets from one another. Besides—she wanted to talk about him. He had filled her mind almost exclusively during that wearisome journey south. Perhaps talking about him would reduce him to his proper place.

"Very odd indeed," she agreed. "Yet I believe he really *is* a farmer. His hands are slender and well-shaped, but they certainly bore signs of rough work, and though we did not actually talk about his farm, he dated various events by referring to crops or seasonal jobs. You know the sort of thing. Where you or I would say, 'That was the year we had the measles,' *he* would say, 'the year the oats did well.' Yes. I think he is

26

certainly a farmer. He is also well educated and well read; and a gentleman. There was nothing of the unlettered rustic in his conversation or his manners."

"A story behind him?" queried Barbara.

"I would think so. Is there not a story behind most of us? Think of ourselves! Few lives are all plain sailing. He may have lost a fortune gaming or suffered losses on 'Change. It was not my place to enquire and he dropped no hints."

"Was he handsome?"

Ann considered that judicially. "He was tall," she said, and Barbara grinned, for this was always her sister's first consideration, "but I would not call him precisely good looking. It was a strong face, a fighting sort of face rather than classically handsome. But he had good teeth—and his nails were well-kept," she ended practically.

Barbara burst out laughing. "You make him sound like a horse," she spluttered. "Teeth and nails indeed! Was he dark or fair?"

"Medium. His hair might show tawny in full sunlight; eyes—a sort of golden hazel." She fell silent for a moment, then said slowly, "I think on the whole I would call him distinguished looking. It sounds ridiculous, doesn't it, for he was quite pathetically shabby—his shirt carefully darned, his coat patched. And yet he looked like *somebody*."

"He certainly seems to have made an impression," said Barbara drily. "From your description I could almost pick him out of a crowd."

And she had no mention of thick curling lashes, gold-tipped, or of the warm intimacy of the gentleman's rare smile. Nor of a clear incisive voice that could suddenly deepen to brooding gentleness. "I should think he might

27

have a hasty temper," she offered meekly, "and would not suffer fools patiently."

"Goes with red hair," agreed her twin laconically. "You say he's a gentleman. And unmarried. Do you think it prudent to entrust yourself to his protection with only this ancient and crotchety retainer to play propriety?"

"Yes," said Ann baldly. "He *is* a gentleman. Not a slimy toad. He'd not lay a finger on me against my will. Though he *did* stipulate"—her eyes began to dance—"that if we came to terms I was not to set about my unwanted admirers with candlesticks or other lethal weapons, since he could not spare the time to be attending court to beg me off."

The man sounded dangerously attractive thought Barbara, her heart sinking. "So on the whole you liked him," she summed up.

"I don't know. Yes, I think so. I would rather say that I was inclined to trust him, that I felt sorry for him, and that I admired his attitude in the face of difficulty. Goodness knows he has problems enough, but he spoke of them lightly, almost amusingly. It made me want to help him, far more than if he'd pulled a long face. And he was truly concerned about his old housekeeper, which I thought unusual. And then, of course, he thinks I shall prove incapable, or weaken and fall by the wayside. I couldn't possibly draw back at this stage."

No, thought Barbara, groaning inwardly. It wouldn't be the first time that Ann got herself entangled in the cause of some lame dog. One or two of them had even been genuine. All of them had brought trouble, expense or anxiety. This one sounded genuine though, and Ann, at twenty-four, was not quite so naive as Ann at thirteen or fourteen. Her experiences in the 'sheltered' life of a governess in genteel families had at least taught her to distinguish pinchbeck from gold. But if she thought she could help this particular lame dog, she would go, and possible difficulties would only make her the more eager. Barbara could only hope that the promised letter of reference would never arrive.

The days of waiting passed slowly and Barbara did not again revert to the subject. Once or twice she ventured to draw her sister's attention to situations that she thought desirable. Ann read the advertisements with polite interest and went on sewing caps. As a further gesture of defiance she also went out and bought herself a copy of Dr. Kitchiner's 'Cook's Oracle', which invaluable work she diligently perused when sewing palled.

Miss Vestey was in the habit of looking through the post bag herself to ensure that none of her charges received anything of a clandestine or forbidden nature, a duty which she performed punctually at six o'clock each evening. The knowledge that her eagerly awaited letter might be lying unnoticed on Miss Vestey's table was tantalizing beyond endurance. It drove Ann out to take long walks, despite the inclement weather. Spring was a tardy arrival this year. She wondered if snow was still lying on the Yorkshire fells.

She spent an afternoon of pouring rain in the library, where she studied Jeffery's Yorkshire Atlas and Colonel Paterson's Road Book, trying to establish the exact position of High Garth. It was hopeless. Mr. Delvercourt had spoken of isolation, of a sad lack of arable land and of being a long way from the nearest church. But there were a great many places that fulfilled all these conditions. Her studies did, however, convince her that, in going to High Garth, she would be venturing into a country far wilder, far more desolate than she had realized. She found the prospect exhilarating.

By the time that she had spent a week under Miss Vestey's roof, courtesy on both sides was growing distinctly threadbare. It was questionable which lady was the more thankful when Miss Vestey was at last able to inform her erstwhile pupil that there were two letters for her. She sincerely wished the girl well, but she found her energy exhausting. Surely *one* of the letters would bring the offer of a suitable post? Both were written on good quality paper, and superscribed in educated, if vastly differing hands. Privately she entertained the hope that Ann would open them in her presence and let fall some hint of their contents, but here she was disappointed. Ann simply accepted them, thanked her politely, and retreated to the privacy of Barbara's room.

Two letters; one addressed in a fine Italian hand, precise and elegant; the other in bold black characters so forceful and impatient that in places the quill had dug into the paper. Which to open first? Childishly she shut her eyes tight and shuffled them about in her hands, put one down on the table and opened her eyes to discover that she had selected the Italian hand. She opened it carefully with Barbara's paper knife, which was just as well, because the first thing that fell out was a bank note for ten pounds. She stared at it as though it might bite, then put it carefully aside and unfolded the letter.

The Reverend Hugh Linthwaite begged to assure Miss Beverley that she need have no hesitation in accepting employment in the household of Mr. Patrick Delvercourt. The gentleman had been known to him for many years. He came of a much respected family and his moral integrity was of a high order. Since he understood that the difficulties of the situation had already been explained to her, he had taken the liberty of making the necessary arrangements for her journey.

These he proceeded to outline in careful detail. She was to travel by Mail, changing at Leeds to the Royal Union which would take her as far as Settle. She was to spend the night of 31 March at the Golden Lion in that town, where accommodation had been reserved for her, and arrangements would be made for her to be conveyed to High Garth on the following day. Funds to cover the expenses of travel were enclosed.

For just one moment Ann felt as Sinbad must have done when he tied himself to the leg of the Great Roc. It seemed that she was now pledged irrevocably to this adventure. The money lying on the table was the sign of it.

She drew a deep breath and broke the seal of the second letter. This was brief. The writer expressed the hope that by the time that she received it she would already have heard from the Reverend Linthwaite and would be willing to accept the arrangements made for her. The final stage of the journey, he warned, would be tedious. It could be considerably shortened if she was willing to ride the last five miles, carrying only such necessities as would go in a saddle bag, since the road was unsuitable for wheeled vehicles at this time of year, being little more than a bridle track. Her other baggage must go round by road and might be delayed for a day or two. Unless the weather turned awkward, in which case it might be a week or more. The choice was hers—save that it depended largely on the weather. But, he added, on a caustic note already familiar, she might as well accustom herself to *that* factor at the outset. If she stayed long enough at High Garth she would soon learn that the weather ruled everything. Meanwhile she was urgently needed. If, after this period for reflection, she could bring herself to face the rigours of which she had been warned, he would look forward to an early meeting. In which sincere hope he was hers, etc., Patrick Delvercourt.

THREE

Travelling, even in the superior comfort of the Mail, gave one too much time for reflection, decided Ann. At first it had been restful, after all the fuss and bustle of departure, to sit back quietly in the knowledge that the die was cast. There had been much last minute shopping to be done—until Barbara enquired tartly if she thought she was bound for Robinson Crusoe's island, such a stock of small necessities as she was purchasing. There had been a final appeal—unsupported by Miss Vestey—to abandon the whole enterprise, return the money and say that she had found other employment. She had stood firm, despite one or two secret qualms. The cost of the journey dismayed her. She could not, in common honesty, allow her employer to invest so large a sum to no purpose. Even if she found conditions at High Garth really intolerable, she would have to endure somehow until her conscience allowed that he had value for his money.

She would almost have preferred to travel by stage. The financial burden would have been less frightening. But it was kind in him to have taken thought for her comfort, and it had done something to reassure Barbara.

Patrick. The name suited him, she thought. For all his shabbiness and his poverty he had the bearing of a patrician and the instincts of one. The well-to-do Anstruthers had thought it quite sufficient to buy her a ticket for the stage. Not Mr. Delvercourt. People of a carping disposition might say that *he* was anxious to secure her services while the Anstruthers were only anxious to be rid of her, but she knew very well that this was not the reason. He was of the breed that would always ensure a woman's comfort and safety to the best of his ability, even at the cost of personal sacrifice. Why! Ten pounds was almost six months salary!

Salary. That was another uncomfortable thought, one that had never troubled her before. She had a living to earn, and so that she did her conscientious best the thought of taking payment for her services had never oppressed her. This time it did. And not because she guessed that her new employer could ill afford it. Always, before, she had worked for strangers. Oh—there had usually been a formal interview at the register office, but to all intents and purposes, strangers. And she could not feel that Mr. Delvercourt was a stranger. For one short evening they had been, if not friends, at least fellow travellers and equals. Now he would be her master. He would be kind and considerate she felt sure, even if he *had* the hasty temper she had mentioned to Barbara, but she must do his bidding submissively and without argument and then, each quarter, accept payment at his hands. Why

34

should the prospect be distasteful? From what he had told her she was likely to work hard enough for her money!

What of her rash promise to see Barbara married? That, too, would depend upon Mr. Delvercourt's good will. Was September a busy season on a Yorkshire farm? Barbara having no mother to arrange matters, the marriage was to take place at Mickleford Hall, and that was only in Lancashire. Not so *very* far away, she thought hopefully. And surely by September she would have proved her worth—or been dismissed. If she gave satisfaction a brief holiday might be permitted her when she explained the circumstances. If she didn't—

Two days of almost continuous travel left her dazed with weariness. At Leeds she had an hour to wait for the coach that would carry her northwards. There was time not only to order refreshments but actually to consume them, and two large cups of coffee and a slice of gingerbread did much to revive her drooping spirits. By the time that she had washed her hands and face and tidied her hair she felt almost herself again and able to take some interest in the passing scene. She had travelled this same road before on her journey south but had been able to see very little, not having been fortunate enough to secure a corner seat and the window, in addition, being largely obscured by mud and sleet. Today, with pale spring sunlight illumining the bare fields, one could see for miles. They changed horses in Skipton, for the last time so far as she was concerned, and pulled briskly up the High Street, catching a glimpse of the lovely old church with the Clifford castle standing sentinel beside it. This was a sound team. They went at their work with good heart, and just as well that they were fine strengthy beasts, thought Ann, for now the character of the countryside was changing. Before Skipton it had been open hill country. Now it was growing wilder, almost mountainous. And there were faintly outlined shapes to the north and west that promised even greater magnificence. She stared about her eagerly. They had passed through one or two villages, quiet places with little sign of life, drawn in upon themselves.

"All gone to Settle for t'market," volunteered a sturdy yeoman who had boarded the coach in Skipton. "It's been the horse fair. I'd ha' been there miself if I'd not had word to go to Kendal on a matter o' business. Stopping off i' Settle is ta? Ye'll find t'place fair throng wi' folk."

In fact they soon began to meet small knots of people coming away from the market. A rider on a stolid brown gelding was the first to pass them, a led filly, presumably a new purchase, following, half reluctant, half skittish. There was a gig piled high with bundles and one or two groups of humbler folk trudging on foot, one man pushing a barrow laden with sacks of meal, another trying to control the strayings of half a dozen geese. Ann wondered if the folk at High Garth patronized the Settle market and if she would find herself faced with such problems as these. When she had so confidently boasted of her domestic capabilities she had forgotten that her marketing had been learned in London. The possibility of having to drive one's dinner home before preparing it had not occurred to her!

This must be Settle itself, for there was that 'monstrous limestone rock called Castleberg, which threatens destruction to the town at its foot'. Her library browsings had prepared her for it, but was certainly an impressive sight. She caught glimpses of one or two substantial houses. Then the horses were checking, swinging righthanded into a narrow arched entrance. She had arrived.

The landlady greeted her politely but with a certain reserve. Young ladies travelling alone were so rare as to be slightly suspect, and in the rush of business consequent upon the horse fair Mrs. Hartley had momentarily forgotten Miss Beverley's impending arrival. When Ann rather shyly gave her name and said that she understood that a room had been reserved for her, the landlady hastened to make amends, explaining frankly how she had come to forget and herself escorting the guest to a comfortably furnished bedchamber. It was not very big and it overlooked the stables at the back of the inn, "But it'll be much quieter than the rooms at the front," she was told. "Fair night's a bit noisy, and a good long sleep in a warm bed is what you'll be wanting most after all that jolting about in the coach. I'll have one of the lasses bring you some hot water and light a fire. Evenings are keen still. And if I was you, miss, I'd have your dinner comfortably up here. I'll see you get a good one, for I daresay you've not had a proper dinner since you left home."

Ann accepted the suggestion gratefully. She would have liked to see something of the town, but it was already dusk. There might be an opportunity for sightseeing in the morning.

By the time that she had exchanged her soiled and crumpled travelling dress for a warm wrapper she had begun to realize the full extent of her own weariness. The fire was blazing up cheerfully, its warmth and its little dancing flames exercising a narcotic effect. When Mrs. Hartley came bustling in with the dinner tray her guest was already half asleep.

The landlady had no notion of letting her good cooking be wasted. She put down the tray with a thump calculated to wake the sleeper and then proceeded to make up the fire, talking briskly the while until she saw the girl started on her meal. The succulence of a portion of duckling, roasted to perfection, the piping hot vegetables and her own cunningly seasoned gravy could be trusted to do the rest.

"And Mr. Delvercourt said to offer you a glass of wine, miss, though if you'd rather have tea or coffee, it's no trouble," she said presently. "Oh yes! And to say that he'd come for you about ten o'clock in the morning and not to forget to put on your riding dress if it's a fine day. Which it will be, by the looks o' yon sky," she concluded sagely.

Ann put down her fork. "Is Mr. Delvercourt in Settle, then?" she asked, surprised.

"Well, in Giggleswick, miss, which is much the same thing, seeing there's naught but the river between them. Lying at the Black Horse tonight." In deference to his notions of propriety, she shrewdly guessed, but lest the guest might consider his choice to be a reflection on the Golden Lion's hospitality she explained, "He wanted the mare shod and he always takes her to Thomas Coar on Bel Hill, so I suppose he thought it'd be handier. He'd have been here earlier but for that. Still, you'll not be sorry for the chance of a good long lie."

"How far is it to High Garth?" asked Ann.

"All of fifteen miles—maybe more—and no kind of a road after you turn off the pike. It's wild country up there. Pretty enough in the summer time, but there's weeks and weeks in the winter when no one can get in or out. Snow comes early and lies late in those parts."

Fortunately, before she could paint any more

38

gloomy pictures of life at High Garth, she was summoned away to deal with some crisis in the kitchen. She returned to bring a dish of curd cakes—a Yorkshire speciality—and the coffee that Ann had preferred, but stayed only long enough to commend the bed—"all good clean feathers from my own geese", to venture a mild pleasantry about there being nothing like the Croft Closes geese, whether for eating or sleeping, and to bid her guest goodnight.

Perhaps there really was some special quality about those goose feathers; perhaps it was just the restorative virtue of a good meal and twelve hours unbroken sleep. But Ann woke in tearing spirits and ravenously hungry, much to Mrs. Hartley's satisfaction. Over breakfast she was assured that it would be perfectly proper for her to stroll out into the sunshine and see something of the town. She found it a quaint, attractive little place, somehow rather French in appearance with its sunny, market square and picturesque houses. It was beautifully situated, close-cupped by green hills, the great rock of Castleberg dominating all. The Tolbooth was disappointing, little better than a ruin. Mrs. Hartley had told her that plans were afoot to pull it down and build a fine new Town Hall. The curious building that occupied the eastern side of the square must be the Shambles. Mrs. Hartley had shown her a sketch of it, drawn by an artistic lady visitor. She studied it with interest. A row of small shops had been built over basement workshops, and on top of these again were tiny houses. You could look down into the area well and watch the craftsmen at work, or you could climb over it by curious little stepped bridges to reach the shops. She bought some bulls eyes for Philip, chiefly for the pleasure of shopping in so novel a fashion.

A small boy followed her up the steps, and as she stood tucking the package into her reticule made some request to the shopkeeper in an accent so broad that she could not understand it. Then, as the man turned to take a jar from the shelf the boy called out, "Apri' Fool," and took to his heels, hooting with laughter as he leapt the last three steps to the street. The shopman shook a threatening fist but grinned companionably at Ann.

"Lads! Ee well—Ah weren't same way mysen at his age!"

She had forgotten the date. All Fools' Day. And living up to its name. For this was a day stolen from summer, warm enough to fool one into believing that winter had fled, with no hint of the bitter winds, the driving snow blizzards that might yet sweep these smiling uplands. And it would not do to be lingering here at the risk of keeping her new employer waiting.

She went back to the inn and changed into riding dress, then finished her packing, setting aside her night gear and a severely plain gown of grey alpaca. It would help her support the character of sober, responsible housekeeper and it would not crease too badly from being packed in a saddle bag. She added two of her new caps to the pile, rolled it up neatly in a shawl and went downstairs to pay her reckoning.

FOUR

Mr. Delvercourt had arrived. She could hear his deep tones and Mrs. Hartley's responsive chuckle as she went sedately down the stairs, her long skirt gathered in one hand. Excitement was quickening her pulses but she managed her greeting composedly enough and gave satisfactory answers to his polite enquiries about her journey. He was carrying two leather satchels, one of which he held out to her, asking if it would be sufficient to hold her gear. Mrs. Hartley summoned an abigail to run up to Miss's room and see. The girl presently returning with the bag neatly strapped up Mrs. Hartley took the second one from Mr. Delvercourt and made to go kitchenwards. To Ann's murmured enquiry about her reckoning she said that the gentleman had already settled it, and bustled away.

"I was early," he explained when she protested, "and thought to save time. And since I want to call at the smithy in Giggleswick on our way home we must not loiter. Shall we go and make sure that the porter has stowed all your belongings in the buggy? I would hate it to reach High Garth only to discover that some indispensable had been left behind."

They strolled out into the inn yard. The vehicle standing there had a capacious boot, which was just as well since it was already heaped with a motley collection of goods. While Mr. Delvercourt helped the porter to bestow the baggage so that the weight was evenly distributed, Ann studied the buggy with interest. It was exceedingly shabby as to paintwork and upholstery, but the harness was well-kept, and if the sturdy brown mare between the shafts laid no claim to high breeding, she looked to be in prime condition. She rolled an inquisitive eye at Ann and accepted her overtures of friendship with affable condescension.

Mr. Delvercourt tipped the porter, the coins slipping easily from palm to palm. Ann wondered why men always seemed to perform this necessary office so easily, while females made much to-do of it. As he turned to help her up into the buggy, Mrs. Hartley came hurrying out with the second saddle bag and a caution to Mr. Delvercourt to mind and keep it the right way up. Then they were off.

"We follow the turnpike as far as Ingleton," explained her escort as they left the market square. "But I have to collect Philip's pony first. I bought it at the fair yesterday—a long-standing promise—and then discovered this morning that it had a shoe loose. So I left it with the smith while I came for you. It's only a step out of our way, and it's a pretty village—if you've not had your fill of scenery these past few days."

He was negotiating the bridge over a swift flowing river as he spoke. Ann smiled, her gaze lifting to the blue-grey bulk of Penyghent that guarded the valley to the north. "Not of such scenery as this," she returned. "I have seen nothing like it. For though it is wild, magnificent, it is somehow reassuring and homely too. It does not overawe the spirit as do, say, the Pyrenees."

He was a little surprised, not having thought so young a female, and one, moreover, in humble circumstances, would have travelled so far afield, but as they had now reached the smithy he was unable to pursue the subject. He handed her the reins and jumped down.

The pony was hitched to a ring by the mounting block. In his thick winter coat he looked a shaggy rolypoly little creature, but he was clearly well used to being handled and made no objection to being fastened behind the buggy.

"I'll lead Maggy through the village," said Mr. Delvercourt. "She's not used to this sort of caper. Best see how she takes it."

Since the road went down a steep hill and turned sharply to the right, his passenger was grateful for this sensible precaution. They passed a beautiful old church and some pretty cottages, crocuses already flaunting their purple and gold in the tiny gardens, crossed a bridge over a gurgling beck, and that seemed to be about all there was of Giggleswick. Mr. Delvercourt, pointing with his whip, told her that a mile or so up *that* road lay Croft Closes, Mrs. Hartley's farm.

"She manages a *farm* as well as an inn?" exclaimed Ann. "And she says her husband is very much an invalid. Yet she is so friendly and so cheerful!"

"She's a good woman, and a brave one," agreed Mr. Delvercourt. And then, on a lighter note, "And a heaven-sent cook. Maggy doesn't seem to mind the

43

pony, does she? One never knows with horses. She has the kindest disposition but she's full of curiosity. Perhaps she has decided to postpone investigations until they meet in the seclusion of the stable."

It was a very mild pleasantry, but Ann giggled. It was such a perfect day, and she had nothing to do but enjoy it in sympathetic company. Mr. Delvercourt didn't talk much. His conversation was typified by a jerk of the head and a laconic "Giggleswick Scars. Limestone quarries," but somehow she knew that he was enjoying the sight of that impressive escarpment as much as she was.

Soon after they rejoined the turnpike he stopped the buggy to show her a roadside well. It looked to her like a perfectly ordinary drinking trough until she noticed that the level of the water was falling. While they watched, it slowly began to rise again. Her guide told her that this was the famous Ebbing and Flowing well, and that people came from miles around to see it.

When he had helped her back into the buggy he did not resume his own seat but handed over the reins once more. "Buckhaw Brow next," he explained, "and a hard haul for Maggy. Let her take it gently, and I'll walk to lighten the load."

Evidently his consideration for people—even people so unimportant as a housekeeper or a governess—was also extended to animals. "Could you not lead her? I would gladly walk too," exclaimed Ann impulsively, as the curve of the road revealed the extent of the hill.

"Best save your energies," he smiled back at her. "Once we turn off the pike there are several places where we must walk and lead the horses. High Garth is well named. The top of the pass is some fifteen hundred feet above sea level, though the farm itself is lower."

44

Ann stared at him wide-eyed. "Goodness! Well you did tell me it was isolated but you didn't say it was on a mountain side."

"It doesn't make a great deal of difference to the working of the place," he assured her. "Just makes it more difficult of access." He chuckled suddenly, and turned a face alight with laughter to hers. "It is to be hoped you like your new situation, Miss Beverley, for if you don't, you will find it extremely difficult to leave it!"

He looked so different, so much younger, the lines of care and cynicism briefly erased by laughter, that she forgot all about their relative positions as employer and servant and yielded to the strange sweet exhilaration that filled her. "Are you suggesting that I should turn back before it is too late?" she said gaily. "I'm not so chicken hearted, I promise you. As for your mountains—I told you—they seem friendly, reassuring. *They* will not frighten me away."

His laughter faded. His voice was sober as he said. "You are seeing them in benign mood. Make no mistake, Miss Beverley, our mountains can be killers, relentless to those who treat them lightly. And there are caves and sinkholes that—But no matter for that. It need not concern us, since, while you are in my household you will not leave the valley without my knowledge and approval."

It was the first touch of the curb. Resentment rose within her, even while she conceded that he was concerned only for her safety. She fell silent. Mr. Delvercourt, leading his mare up Buckhaw Brow, quite unconscious that he had given offence, wondered if any other girl had ever looked so much like spring incarnate. At their first meeting he had thought her good-looking if not strictly beautiful. But he had seen

45

her only by candle light and so he had not allowed for a skin that, in this stark, revealing sunshine, was flawless. Though little given to fanciful hyperbole he found himself thinking of the petals of a wild rose. And the eager light in the big brown eyes was delightful.

It was a line of thought that must be sternly checked. It was the girl's capability, her industry that mattered, not her appearance. Whenever he had looked back to that chance meeting at the Pheasant, he had felt considerable misgiving, guiltily aware that he had allowed himself to be influenced by an evening spent in congenial company—the first for many months. They had talked of books, of ideas, of new inventions and a changing world. And such talk had been to him like a cup of cool water to a man foundering in a desert. He knew that it had caused him to reverse his first judgement and to offer Miss Beverley employment. Riding home in the bleak dawn he had been amazed at his own folly. To put such a girl in a hill farm and expect her to cope with its heavy work was like putting a thoroughbred mare to the plough. He must have been mad! But he had given his word and he would stick by it.

Now his doubts came back in full force. The position was already difficult enough. If he were to find himself physically attracted to his new housekeeper, it would become impossible. And in her neat dark green habit, with that look of delighted anticipation on her flower-like face, she was a sight to quicken any man's pulses.

He climbed soberly back to his place when they reached the top of the hill and steadied the mare on the long descent in silence. But sober thoughts were alien to the glory of this perfect day. The very air was like wine. He could see his companion savouring it, almost swallowing it, in great gulps. Mr. Delvercourt yielded to temptation, decided to enjoy his exceptional holiday to the full, and put care from him.

There were several miles of good turnpike road, and every bend revealed new and even lovlier vistas. There were early primroses peeping from the banks, a haze of greenery over the larches, and lapwings wheeling in their courtship display overhead. Maggy was well content to plod along steadily, choosing her own gait while her master answered Miss Beverley's eager questions. He regaled her with all the theories, scientific and legendary, as to what caused the Ebbing and Flowing well to ebb and flow. He smiled at her eager exclamations for the beauty of the changing scene. Save for an occasional reminder that this was an unusually early season following upon a mild winter; that sometimes they were still snow-bound at this time of year, and that frosts could be expected as late as May, he said nothing to damp her enthusiasm. Indeed he shared it, was deeply if inarticulately proud of this country of his birth. His warnings were given only lest disappointment should follow this too perfect introduction. By the time they reached the point at which they were to leave the pike, they were getting on famously, the easy companionship into which they had fallen at their first meeting already re-established.

The green track they were to follow branched off by Thornton church. Two horses were tethered to the stocks that stood by the church gate, and the youngster in charge of them, a tall, well-set-up lad of about nineteen or twenty, was amusing himself by sitting in that seat of sinners with out-thrust legs and folded arms. He jumped up when he saw them coming and knuckled an eyebrow to the lady. There was a brief colloquy as the saddle bags were strapped into place. Mr. Delvercourt came over to help Miss Beverley out of the buggy. "And don't forget!" he called over his shoulder. "Put up at Crag Hill overnight if you think Maggy's done enough. They're half expecting you."

The boy nodded understanding and drove off with a twirl of his whip that made Mr. Delvercourt grin. "Young Robert Alder," he said. "A good lad. His father is our nearest neighbour, and no man could want a better. To look at him and to hear him talk you'd think he was as dour as a January frost and close-fisted to boot. But these are his horses we are riding, and offered without so much as a thought. Young Robert is his only son." His face clouded. "There should have been another, but something went amiss. It was in the depth of winter and no one could get in or out to bring help. They both died. He had bred that mare you are riding himself—a gift for his wife. Now Robert lays claim to her and loves her dearly, but he was proud to bring her for you to ride."

The mare was certainly a lovely creature, far superior to the rather clumsy bay that Mr. Delvercourt was bestriding. Even without his explanation it was easy to see that she was someone's cherished pet. She was a delightful ride and sure-footed as any mountain goat. Which was just as well, for the track, to Ann's eyes, was appalling. Quite as bad as some she had known in Spain. It went up and up, twisted back on itself, then submitted to circumstances and climbed again. There was little opportunity for admiring the scenery, though Mr. Delvercourt *did* draw her attention to the majesty of Ingleborough, serenely purple-blue against the paler blue of the sky. "That's the nearest we come to it," he told her. "Whernside—ahead there—is a bit higher but less impressive."

48

Ann grew hot and breathless. Presently they had to dismount and lead the horses. They were very high up now. Occasionally she glanced back at the magnificent view spread behind them. Even under sunshine the dale was a savage, forbidding place, but she took comfort from the sight of the occasional solid looking farmhouse tucked away among its sheltering trees.

Goodness but she was going to be stiff and sore tomorrow, she thought resignedly, toiling steadily upward. It was months since she had ridden, and then only a subdued livery hack in the Park. Today's little jaunt was very different! Climbing this rough track in habit and boots wouldn't help unaccustomed muscles, either. And to think that she had come of her own free will. "Ride the last five miles," indeed! Did the creature call this riding? She would not be so easily cozened next time!

She was very thankful when "the creature" finally called a halt, even though his solemn courtesy as much as the smile in his eyes betrayed the fact that he was very well aware of her feelings.

"We'll turn the horses loose while we eat," he suggested. "Not that there's much grazing for them yet. Will you see to lunch while I unsaddle? Set it out on this rock here, where the spring comes out of the hillside. The wall will shelter us from the breeze and we shall be warm enough in the sun."

Ann forgot both aches and pains and indignation. This was fun. If it was months since she had ridden it was years since she had enjoyed a picnic, and as she unpacked the satchel she saw that Mrs. Hartley's notion of proper provision for such an occasion was designed to tempt a sybarite, let alone healthy young appetites sharpened by exercise and keen moorland air. There were meat pasties, fresh baked that morning, still warm in their napkin. There were eggs boiled hard and cheese and oatcakes, sticky gingerbread and apples, as well as a bottle of lemonade and two horn drinking cups.

Mr. Delvercourt put the bottle in the stream to cool, stretched his long length on the turf, sighed luxuriously and bit into a crisply golden pasty. They ate for a while in companionable silence. So peaceful it was that it seemed almost unreal. Ann began to count the sounds that she could hear. There was the plash of the spring, falling two or three feet into the tiny pool; the occasional sigh of the breeze and the cropping of the horses as they moved nearer; once, faintly, the distant barking of a dog. And that was all. She leaned back against the sun-warmed rock and thought that even the small tearing sound of her teeth biting into an apple seemed loud in that utter stillness. A sensuous pleasure filled her. She might even have drifted into sleep, had not the clear bubbling call of some strange bird broken the spell.

"Goodness! What was that?" she exclaimed, startled.

"Curlew," returned Mr. Delvercourt succinctly. "See —there he goes." A large brownish bird with a long curved beak flapped slowly away down the valley. "They came early this year," he said contentedly.

She looked the question.

"They winter on mud flats in estuaries," he explained. "Their return to the moors is our first harbinger of spring." He scrambled to his feet and went down to the stream for the lemonade. It was cold and delicious and she drank thirstily, demurring politely when he made to replenish the cup until he said that he preferred water. "Especially *this* water, straight from the spring," he added, shaking the drops from his cup and handing it back to her. There was a good deal of food left. He watched her neatly re-packing the satchel with a quizzical eye.

"And now that you have sampled our Dales' cooking —admittedly at its best—do you still feel yourself capable of catering for a hungry household?"

She looked up from her task indignantly, caught the teasing gleam, and said demurely, "I shall do my best to give satisfaction, sir."

He laughed. "I suspect that you will at least give as good as you get," he told her, and went off to catch the horses.

"A pity to leave this delightful spot, but I want to be back for evening milking," he explained as he tightened the girths and secured the saddle bags. "I've enjoyed my holiday, but on a farm that usually means that others have been doing my work. So if you're rested, Miss Beverley, we'll push on. We have quite a distance to walk before it is reasonable to mount again."

The track had begun to descend, dropping sharply at times but eventually settling down into a sunken lane. They could ride abreast now and it was easier to talk. Ann's questions about the farm came thick and fast. Mainly sheep, he told her. They kept a few cows —there were seven at the moment—to supply their own needs and make butter and cheese for the market. Any surplus went to fatten the pigs. They grew as much hay as possible and turnips for winter feed. No. No oats nowadays. Too chancey a crop at this altitude. They might do well in a good summer, but good summers were rare. She was just going to enquire about a vegetable garden when he said quietly, "There is High Garth. You can just see the chimneys through the

51

trees. We shall lose it again as the lane swings away, but we are nearly home."

The approach to the farm was a short track leading from the lane. Some attempt had been made to improve the surface by filling in the worst holes with small stones and ramming them down as smoothly as possible. Ann remembered the smooth well-kept drive at the Anstruther's. Remembered, too, that it had been forbidden to the governess, who was expected to use the side door in her comings and goings, and reserved judgement.

The house itself looked surprisingly commodious. It was long and low and built of local stone. They came first to a barn-like building which Mr. Delvercourt called a laithe. Adjoining this was the house itself. Ann had a brief impression of small twinkling window panes, a low stone porch sheltering the front door and a narrow strip of garden where a few crocuses and daffodils peeped bravely through a tangle of dead stuff that should have been cleared in autumn.

"The stable is at the back," said Mr. Delvercourt, and she followed him obediently round the end of the house into a small yard roughly paved with stone flags. As he swung down from his horse a small boy came hurtling from the back of the house and flung himself upon him.

"Did you buy me a pony?" demanded an excited voice.

"Philip, Philip! Manners, my child! Here is Miss Beverley travelled all this way to look after us all and teach you your lessons, and all you can do is babble about ponies. Make your bow like a gentleman, if you please."

The child turned reluctantly to do his bidding. Ann wondered a little that Mr. Delvercourt should so far

52

have forgotten his own childhood as to expect proper courtesy from an over-excited child. But it would never do to begin by questioning his methods of training, so she slid down to the ground, looped the rein over her arm and acknowledged the introduction with due formality.

By this time Mr. Delvercourt had turned away to speak to a middle aged man who had suddenly materialized from nowhere and was leaning on the yard wall explaining something about, "t'strawberry roān". Philip was dancing up and down with impatience but the slow-spoken rustic was absorbing all his brother's attention.

"Yes, Philip," said Ann, suddenly making up her mind. "He did indeed buy you a pony, and it seems a great shame that I should have seen him before you did. But your brother will tell you all about him when he is less occupied. And I think our first lesson will have to be about some of the famous horses of history. There are a great many of them, you know, and they have some splendid sounding names. You might like to name your pony for one of them, though I must confess he doesn't look quite like a Pegasus or a Bucephalus. You will have to get to know him before you decide."

The child's face cleared magically. "Patrick *said* you were a reg'lar right 'un," he told her earnestly. "Will you make us puddings and cakes? And *not* say I have to eat up my meat if it's fat?"

"I *like* making cakes and puddings," Ann told him, carefully avoiding the vexed question of fat meat. "Which are your favourites?"

But Philip was scarcely launched on what promised to be an exhaustive catalogue when a deep amused voice said gently, "I thought you laid no claim to the knack of managing small children, Miss Beverley. Yet

53

here is Philip who, I may tell you, is strongly opposed to the idea of education, already—almost literally, in fact—eating out of your hand."

Ann looked slightly guilty. "I'm afraid I stole your thunder, sir. Since you were so busy, I told him that you *had* bought him a pony. Which naturally predisposed him in my favour. The idea that his first lessons should be about horses also took well, while cakes and puddings to a small boy"—

He smiled. "Let us see if you show equal skill in dealing with Janet's prejudices," he suggested, and lifted the latch and stood aside for her to precede him into the kitchen.

FIVE

It was a long low-pitched room, and even on this bright afternoon the light was dim, save immediately under the windows. It had a heavily beamed ceiling that caused its owner to duck his head with the unconscious familiarity of long usage, and the floor was stone flagged and innocent of any covering save for a home made list rug in gay colours that was spread in front of the fire.

So much Ann had time to notice before she realized that someone was sitting in the high-backed chair that was drawn up to the fire. She heard the click of knitting needles but the knitter had her back to them and obviously had not heard them come in. Mr. Delvercourt crossed to the hearth saying, "Here we are at last, Janet. Had you given us up?" He raised his voice a little, and Ann realized that Janet must be hard of hearing.

She was considerably startled to see that the old

lady who now rose to greet them was wearing a black silk gown that, save for its out-moded style, would not have demeaned a Duchess, and had further embellished her appearance by donning a beautifully laundered lace cap and putting a heavy gold locket about her throat. It was plain to be seen that Janet was very much on her dignity and did not take kindly to the notion of being superseded by some impudent upstart wench. She had summoned all the resources of her wardrobe to her aid in her determination to depress the intruder's pretensions. It was an attitude that evoked Ann's sympathy, even while she knew that it might make things difficult for her. After all—who would want to be shown, however kindly, that they were past useful work?

She acknowledged her introduction to Mistress Howson with quiet courtesy but waited for the older woman to take the conversational lead. But it was Mr. Delvercourt who plunged into the breach, saying in a puzzled voice, "You're very fine today, Janet. Don't tell me I've forgotten your birthday again!"

"I put on my best to honour to Miss Beverley's coming," said Janet stiffly.

Instinct warned Patrick that the next half hour might be a little awkward. It was no place for a mere male. "And very becomingly you look," he told her. "But *I* must go and shed my respectable clothes and get into working rig. I'll leave Miss Beverley in your charge."

Left to their own devices, the two eyed each other warily. "You'll take a cup of tea, Miss Beverley?" enquired Janet primly.

"Oh, please!" said Ann. "Do you know, it is the best part of a week since I last enjoyed a cup of tea. In the posting inns it is much safer to order coffee. When

56

Mistress Hartley offered me tea last night I had not realized that hers would probably be drinkable."

There was the faintest discernible thaw in Janet's attitude. "Yes, you could trust Isabella Hartley. A gradely woman and a rare cook." She went competently about the business of filling the kettle at a pump over the sink, proudly pointing out the advantage of having water laid on to the kitchen, "Mr. Patrick had it done after we were frozen up for two months one winter," hanging the kettle on a hook over the fire and setting out two cups of a delicacy that seemed oddly out of place in this workaday setting. "And you can safely trust *my* tea," she told the newcomer. "It's one luxury that Mr. Patrick insists upon, though I doubt me that's mainly for my sake, for it's rarely he drinks it himself." Her lips snapped shut on that, as though already she feared she had unbent too far.

Ann knew better than to offer assistance, or even to comment on Janet's remarks, in so far as they concerned her master. It seemed safer to speak of tea. "If the tea is worthy of these cups, it will be the finest tea I ever tasted," she said, lifting one carefully in both hands to examine it more closely.

"Brought back by Mr. Patrick's grandpa, so he says, from eastern parts where the tea grows," volunteered Janet, pleased, and poured hot water into a clumsy earthenware teapot. She waved it under Ann's gaze before tipping the water into the slopstone. "Those fine chaney cups are well enough for drinking, but there's nothing like *this* for making a good brew."

They drank their tea in the appreciative silence which, as Janet had indicated, was its due, Ann studying the big farm kitchen with frank interest and occasionally stealing a covert glance at her companion. Since Janet seemed disinclined for talk, she too kept

57

silence. Moreover she was beginning to feel a trifle daunted at the magnitude of the task that she had so light-heartedly undertaken. There was so little here that was familiar. The furniture was sparse—a large, well-scrubbed table in the middle of the room, a high-backed oak settle, three windsor chairs and a couple of roughly made stools pushed back against one wall and two large meal arks ranged against another. These latter were much superior to the chairs and stools, being beautifully made and even decorated with a simple carved leaf design.

The focal point of the room was the huge, deeply recessed hearth, and it was this that Ann found the most alarming, for of all the equipment standing within it or arranged on shelves and hooks at either side, the only things she recognized were the bellows, a Dutch oven and what she took to be an antiquated roasting spit. For the rest, the very pans looked strange, solid heavy iron where she had been accustomed to copper. The strings of onions, the bunches of dried herbs and a side of bacon hanging from a beam at the far end of the room were reassuring, but she had never dreamed that she would be expected to cook on an open fire. Not even a coal fire, at that. They seemed to burn some kind of turf. How did one manage about bread and pies and cake? There was something that looked like an oven door set in the wall at one side of the fire, but how in the world was it heated? By the time that she had drunk her tea, the future bristled with unforeseen difficulties. She began to wonder how long it would be before she was dismissed for sheer incompetence.

"I daresay you'll be wanting to change your gown," said Janet presently. "Yours is the room facing you at the head of the stair. You'll find water for washing in the jug, but there's a sup of warm left in the kettle if you choose to carry it up."

But Ann declined the offered luxury, rightly suspecting that it would be taken as evidence of Southron softness.

The bedroom was shiningly clean but very bare, and at the moment strongly redolent of beeswax. The narrow pallet was covered with a patchwork quilt which contributed a welcome touch of colour to scrubbed boards and whitewashed walls. There was a three drawer dressing chest with a standing mirror and a jug and basin jostling each other on top of it, and a stool with a padded seat. Closer investigation revealed that the sheets, though old, were snowy white and lavender scented, and that a feather bed had been laid on top of the straw mattress. The one window was small and was not made to open, but Ann guessed that this might well be an advantage in these northern heights. It gave her a magnificent prospect of the dale, and, deeply recessed in the thickness of the wall, formed an alcove of golden light so dense that you felt you could scoop it up in handfuls like water.

But this was not the time to be indulging in whimsical fancies. Hastily she unpacked her belongings, shook out the grey alpaca and laid it on the bed. Her hair would have to do. It would take too long to brush it out and re-braid it, but luckily her cap would cover it. She stripped off her habit, washed her hands and face and dressed again as quickly as possible, putting her few possessions in one of the drawers and hanging her habit on a peg behind the door. A swift glance in the mirror assured her that she looked reasonably neat. She wondered if Janet would be willing to lend her an apron until her other luggage arrived. Then, with an unconscious stiffening of her shoulders, she went down to the kitchen again.

She had need of all her resolution. As Janet led her from room to room, pointing out such items of interest as a mill for grinding corn, a stand churn and a cheese press, her heart sank lower and lower. It was not that she had boasted her capabilities without good grounds. She *was* well trained in household management. She was even pretty well acquainted with dairy work, since Papa Fortune had removed his household into the country every summer. He had a rather pretentious residence in Hertfordshire—very gothic—but possessing the advantage of its own home farm. Here his two step-daughters had been set to learn how to dress poultry, to milk the cows and to make butter and cheese. And Ann, despite her resentment of this tyrannical disposition of her time and her energies, had secretly rather enjoyed the change from the monotonous routine of the town house.

But even in the country she had never been called upon to handle such primitive equipment as this. Why! That stone cheese press was so vast it had an alcove all to itself, and looked as though it would take two men to lift it. Papa Fortune, nip-farthing that he was in many ways, had never begrudged money spent on up-to-date domestic appliances. He had been one of the first to install a Rumford closed stove in his town house, and then, satisfied of its efficiency, had ordered another for the Hertfordshire place, boasting that not only did it save coals, but that he had also reduced the expenses of his establishment by dispensing with the services of an under cook and a scullery maid.

Her response to Janet's explanations grew more and more stilted, and as the old woman opened the door that led from the dairy to the yard she saw that the girl's pretty, apple blossom colouring had faded and that she looked quite frightened. Beneath her severe appearance, Janet's heart was warm and tender to all young creatures. If, on this one occasion, her welcome had been less than cordial, it was because she herself had been afraid. But so far she was quite pleasantly impressed. This was no uppity brass-faced wench, but a young woman of sense and good manners. One, moreover, who didn't mumble her words so that one was for ever asking her to speak up. The prospect of congenial company, especially during the long dark days of winter, seemed suddenly attractive. She said brusquely, but kindly, "But no need to be worrying about cheese making yet awhile. It'll be June before we can make a start, maybe July. And by then you'll be into the way of things."

The girl turned to her swiftly, her face strained, her hands clasped in mute appeal. "If you will help me," she begged, on a note of desperation. "If you will teach me. I can work hard, and truly I can cook and bake as I said. But it is all so strange. I've never been used to an open hearth and I'd be afraid of spoiling the food while I'm learning. But you—if only you would—could show me how to manage."

Deliberate artifice could scarcely have put more potent words into her mouth. Janet would never have been deceived by a pretty pretence of seeking her help and advice. But the near-panic in the young, anxious face was utterly convincing. She capitulated without more ado.

"I might have known Mr. Patrick'd choose a right 'un," was her way of phrasing it, in comical echo of young Philip. "One that doesn't think she knows it all but is willing and eager to learn of her elders. 'Course I'll help you, my lass, and glad to do it. I've not forgot my own first sight of this place. Fair scunnered me it did—and me never a cook any way. But young Robert's mother was alive then, dear kind soul that she was, and *she* put me in the way of things. It's just a knack. You'll soon get accustomed. As for spoiling the food—I'll never forget the first batch of clap-bread I made. We don't often eat wheaten bread. Oats are what we mostly use, both for bread and porridge. Well —I doubt you could have soled your boots with mine, and that's about all it *was* good for. But just you leave that to me to start with, lassie, and you'll soon learn to manage the rest."

So it was that Patrick, coming rather warily into the kitchen after setting the milk pails in the dairy, heard Janet say, "That's it, Miss Ann. Just blow gently or we'll have a smother of dust everywhere. It'll soon be hot enough for the potatoes," and found Ann on her knees plying the bellows, one of Janet's aprons tied over her grey gown and an expression of deep absorption on her face.

"I was just telling Miss Ann that we have to be saving with coals," Janet informed him, "seeing as they have to be packed in from Garsdale. And even then," continuing her exposition, "the ponies can't manage that last steep bit and men have to drag the stuff the rest of the way on sledges. For myself I like a peat fire just as well, now that I've learned how to manage it. And you will, too, Miss Ann, come winter time. Just wait till you come down on a bitter frosty morning. Just a lift with the poker, a puff or two from the bellows, and there's your fire, all ready to boil the kettle. *And* a cosy warm kitchen to greet you. Aye. There's a deal to be said for a peat fire."

"And just wait till you come down on a bitter frosty morning and the damned thing's gone out on you," interpolated Patrick, forgetting to guard his tongue in his delight at the friendly relations that had obviously been established between the pair. He had known it was all right as soon as he heard 'Miss Ann' instead of the formal 'Miss Beverley'. "Nothing but a heap of cold grey ash staring at you and a four foot drift between you and the stick house. She'll just love it then, won't she Janet?"

"And well you know that I always keep a few sticks handy in the bread oven," retorted Janet with dignity. "And it's not seemly, Mr. Patrick, to be using strong language in front of a lady."

He grinned unrepentantly. "Miss Beverley was bred up in military circles," he said cheerfully. "I dare say she has heard worse, despite that demure expression." And as Ann laughed despite herself, went on, "And the children are not here to be corrupted. I left Philip garnishing the pony's stall yet again. He'll be running off with your hearth rug to make it a good warm bed, if you don't watch him. Where are the girls?"

"I sent them off to Far Riggs to wash the bed linen. That's no job for men folk and it was a grand day for the drying. Besides, it's some small return for the loan of Robert and the horses. They went off as merry as grigs. You'd have thought they were going to a fair. But they're good lasses, though it ill becomes me to praise my own kin, and I'll warrant they'll have made a good job of it. They'll be back any minute. Supper'll bring them."

Patrick nodded approvingly. "A good thought, Janet. In that case I'll see to the milk before I clean up for supper."

"That you'll not, sir," exclaimed Janet indignantly. "Miss Ann and me'll do it and plenty of time to spare before supper's ready. Be off with you and leave us to get on in peace."

Ann blinked. It was a strange household she was

63

come to, where a servant, even one so trusted and venerable as Janet, might bespeak the master so. But there was no sharp reprimand. Instead Mr. Delvercourt flung up one arm as of a culprit deflecting a sharp box on the ear and made a laughing escape, while Janet bustled through into the dairy and began to set out the pans into which the milk must be poured. Ann, her hands assisting nimbly with this familiar task, felt that there was a good deal about this remote dales farm that needed further elucidation.

SIX

The next month was the strangest and the busiest that Ann had ever known. She was granted a whole week of the halcyon weather that had marked All Fools' Day, and every minute of it was crammed with new experiences. She learned how to fire the beehive oven that was set in the thickness of the wall, burning the carefully prepared faggots inside the oven itself until the bricks were hot enough, then raking out the glowing embers and putting in the loaves and pies that she had made, though at first she suffered many an anxious moment until the time came to take them out, fearing to find them either scorched or still half raw. She made porridge and broth and stews thick with dumplings in the heavy iron pans hanging over the turf fire. She checked the stores and drew up a list of deficiencies to be made good next time someone went to market, and she tackled the neglected gardens. At one time the kitchen garden had been well stocked.

She discovered rhubarb, already gleaming pink and yellow through last year's dead leaves, and there were currant bushes and raspberry canes breaking into leaf. There was a herb garden, too, where she recognized thyme and sage and rosemary among others. But the vegetable patch was matted with weed, and Patrick, coming upon her unawares, promptly forbade any further attempts to dig it over. One of the men would do that. Then she might plant what she chose. But no more attempting of tasks beyond a girl's strength. If she needed help she was to ask for it, and it would be given as promptly as the overriding demands of farm work permitted. Conscious of blistered palms and an aching back, Ann submitted thankfully.

It had been agreed between them that Philip's lessons should not begin until his preceptress had had a chance to settle into the routine of farmhouse life. This to that young gentleman's vast content, since he was wholly absorbed in his new pony. Patrick had shown him how to feed, water and groom the little creature, threatening dire punishment if rations were exceeded or too many tit-bits given. "A piece of apple or carrot you may give him occasionally," he ended, "so that he knows you are his friend. But the best thing is to talk to him. Keep your voice quiet and your movements steady, so that you don't startle him. I'll give you a hand with the grooming occasionally, but the more you do for him the better he will learn to know you."

Ann, listening, felt once more that he expected a good deal of a small boy. But Philip nodded solemnly and, so far as she could see, followed his brother's instructions to the letter. By the end of the week Jigs —named eventually from the clatter of his small hooves on the flagstones—was following his little master like a dog. They were for ever pushing that questing brown muzzle away from the kitchen door as the pony demanded admission.

When he was not with the pony, Philip attached himself to Ann. He had early discovered that she had a fund of stories at her command. The ones about her own childhood he liked best, because they were "really truly ones". She was knowledgeable about horses, too. But her chief attraction in Philip's eyes lay in her ignorance of High Garth's ways, and her willingness to learn of him. This was an experience that had not previously come his way. With enthusiasm he undertook the role of cicerone, growing in confidence as his first shy explanations were received with respect. Patrick, busy about his work in fields and buildings, sometimes saw the pair pass by, Philip expounding earnestly, pausing to take his companion's hand if he thought the footing treacherous, releasing it to gesture eagerly at some feature of interest, Ann gravely attentive, quite oblivious of his own presence. It seemed to him that good relations were being established in *that* field.

The weather broke. Vicious winds brought hail and sleet and made the kitchen chimney smoke. There was an all-pervading smell of wet clothes and sheep. Two cade lambs were bedded down beside the wide hearth and, as they gathered strength, tumbled about under everyone's feet. The men came in at dusk soaked and chilled and ravenous.

Despite the clutter the lamp-lit kitchen was warmly inviting, the savoury smell issuing from the big kail pot going far to substantiate Ann's claim that she really could cook. Supper was the main meal of the day, the only one that could be enjoyed in anything approaching leisure. The men were often out at first light, returning for a breakfast of porridge and cheese and oatcakes when the morning milking was done and the stock fed. Sometimes Patrick and Will would come in for a bite at mid-day, but Jim, the shepherd, preferred to take a piece of bread and bacon or a mutton pie in one of his capacious pockets. There was enough walking to be done, he said, tewing after his feckless charges, even with Fly's help. Fly was his dog. Ann, who liked dogs, could find little to admire in this specimen, a slinking black and white creature, wall-eyed and muddy coated, save perhaps her loyalty to her master. She was never admitted beyond the back kitchen where she would lie, nose on paws, until Jim went out. Then she was at his heels, shadow-like, without a word spoken. He never praised nor petted her, yet she ignored all others. Ann's own polite overtures were disregarded. The others tried to explain it to her.

"She's a working dog," said Janet. "None of your petted lap-dogs. She's no time for soft soap and compliments."

Patrick made matters a little plainer. "She's Jim's," he said. "He's made her. Raised her from a pup. Wait till you've seen them working together. No, I know he doesn't fuss over her, but I can assure you that there's not money enough in the Mint to buy her, and he'd starve himself rather than let Fly go short."

Even Will, who regarded sheep as vastly inferior creatures, allowed grudgingly that Fly was worth her keep. "That 'un 'ud 'ave made a good cattle dog if she'd been raised right." And that was praise indeed.

In making a place for herself at High Garth, Ann was getting to know its inhabitants in a way denied to casual visitors. She found them puzzling at times. As she had once said to her sister, there was a story behind most people, and she longed to know the stories behind her new friends. Janet had volunteered the information that Jim had been at High Garth longer than any of them, so perhaps it was natural that he should regard it as home and never dream of seeking an easier job in the lowlands. Will was less understandable. He helped wherever he was needed, though the cows were his real interest. Surely he would have been happier on a large farm with a proper dairy herd? He was forthright and inclined to be short-tempered, but he was kindhearted and never bore malice. Jim was much quieter. Indeed, at first, when he was wrapped in one of his brooding silences, Ann thought that he showed about as much sign of intelligence as one of his own sheep. She was to learn that, though his speech was slow and infrequent, he had an age-old wisdom, both acquired and instinctive. His rare pronouncements were well worthy of respect.

Meg and Jenny, the two young maids, were Janet's greatnieces. They were twins, fifteen years old, and thought it quite fascinating that Miss Ann should also be a twin. They never wearied of asking about Barbara, and found it hard to believe that she should be so different from her sister, since they themselves were like as two peas. They had been in Janet's care for nearly three years, since their mother died. Their father was a guard on a mail coach and they were very proud of him. In his scarlet coat with its blue lapels and blue waistcoat and his gold-banded hat, he was a fine figure of a man. You had to be brave to be a guard, they told Ann, and able to shoot at highwaymen if they attacked the mail. Dadda had a bell-mouthed blunderbuss and pistols, too. He did not allow them to touch these fearsome weapons, but he *had* let them blow the long brass horn which signalled the mail's approach.

"But it only made a noise like a sick sheep when *we* blew it," said Jenny regretfully.

"And Dadda can play *tunes* on it," confided Meg, wide-eyed with admiration.

But Dadda's glamourous calling did not permit him to keep a close eye on two growing daughters. "And Margaret—their mother—was dear as a daughter to me," said Janet. "I was full willing to take her girls. Only with Mr. Patrick needing me too, it might have been awkward. But all ended well, as you see. The lassies have taken to farmhouse life like ducks to water. And now that you're here to give an eye to their manners and show them how a proper lady behaves, they couldn't be better placed."

And what claim had Mr. Patrick upon the good soul that might have conflicted with the needs of girls so dearly loved? The very manner of address indicated that Janet had known him in childhood—had probably been his nurse. And this Janet herself eventually confirmed. Though she had taken a strong liking to Miss Beverley and had helped her as much as she could, Janet was a canny Yorkshire woman. Her confidences came slowly, especially where they concerned her adored master.

There had been the business of Mr. Patrick's parlour, for instance. On her first tour of the house, Ann had not even been aware of the existence of this apartment, since its door opened from the small square hall that they never used. If you entered High Garth by the front door you stepped into that hall, and the parlour door lay to your left. Since all the residents used the back door or the entrance through the dairy, it was not for several days that Ann, preoccupied with her new responsibilities, realized that there *was* another room on the ground floor. She had been tidying up in the front garden. Standing back to admire the result of her efforts, she caught sight of Janet polishing windows, and suddenly realized that these windows had curtains, a refinement that was totally lacking elsewhere. Janet, seeing her surprised face, evidently decided that she might now be permitted to enter this sanctum, and asked her help in washing the pieces of china that stood in a small cabinet under the windows.

"For they're family pieces and I've never trusted them to the girls. I always reckon to give this room a good clean in spring. The master doesn't use it in winter to save firing, but he'll sit here sometimes of a Sunday in summer. Maybe he'll let you use it for Master Philip's lessons."

Ann stared about her with interest. The room had both charm and dignity. She remembered the stiff formality of the Anstruther's drawing room. It had been done over in the French Empire style and at vast expense just after she went to them, every piece of its original furniture ruthlessly relegated to humbler rooms. The result might be elegant, but it was cold and unwelcoming. The few pieces in this farmhouse parlour seemed to belong together even if they had not been designed to do so. The gate-legged table was probably Queen Anne if not older, and its oak had the patina that is only bestowed by years of loving polishing. An oak bookcase stood against one wall. But the bureau was walnut, the little china cabinet rosewood and she rather thought that the frames of the two comfortable looking upholstered chairs were sycamore. Yet thee whole effect was harmonious and restful. The clear upland light shining through the windows spared neither faded damask nor well worn carpet, but since the room was wholly unpretentious it didn't seem to matter. It was quite absurd, but she felt a strong desire to tend and cherish these venerabl household gods. Automatically her hand went out t caress the inlay on the bureau.

She said gently, "It is beautiful. No wonder you di not want anyone else to meddle with such lovel things. I will be very careful, I promise."

Over the washing of the ornaments, Janet unben still further. That large blue bowl had belonged to Mr Patrick's uncle. He it was who had bought the farm and had the parlour built on to the original house. H had never married, and after a lifetime spent mainl in foreign travel he had chosen to pass his declinin years in this remote spot. "Dear alone knows why," said Janet, "unless 'twas to be near his sister. His onl surviving kin, she was, and Mr. Patrick's mother. Bu little enough the old man saw of her, choosing to liv at the back of beyond like this and her an invalid eve since Mr. Patrick was born. He'd ride over to th Court now and then to visit her but he never stayed above an hour or so and it generally made trouble. H and the master never saw eye to eye and it was m poor lady that suffered for their disagreements."

She set the blue bowl back in its place and trans ferred her attention to a Chelsea figure. "Though I *wil* say the master never raised any objection to Master Patrick spending his holidays up here with his uncle," she went on slowly, as though arranging her own ideas "Maybe he reckoned the lad would soon weary of his fancy for farming if he saw enough of it. But that was where he missed his guess."

A lady should never betray personal curiosity; nor should she question servants. It now became apparent that, in this respect, Ann was no lady. "Did he wish his son to follow some other career?" she enquired, in a tone which, she hoped, indicated only polite interest.

72

"No need for him to follow any career," said Janet sharply, "save that of tending his father's estates and succeeding in good time to his father's place."

Ann concentrated on the careful drying of some Worcester tea cups, and waited hopefully.

"They're a queer thrawn lot, the Delvercourts," said the old woman reflectively. "And Mr. Henry—that's Mr. Patrick's father—one of the worst. Not that he hadn't his good side," she added fairly, "but obstinate! Nay! That's too genteel a word. Downright pig-headed I'd call him. Once he took a notion there was no moving him. The mistress used to make excuses for him. She'd talk to me a lot, nights, when she couldn't sleep and I'd sit with her. Wonderful chief we were together, for she'd no one else to talk to, poor lady. It came of him being a younger son, she would explain. And being a cripple made it worse. Not that he was much of a cripple, but he'd a hip injury from a child that made him walk lame, and one shoulder was higher than the other. He could get about pretty well, but walking or riding he always looked ungainly and it irked his pride. So he was determined to make a stir in the world by hedge or by stile. Maybe if Miss Ellen had been well and strong she could have coaxed him out of his odd fancies, and certain it is he got worse after she died."

She began to replace the various pieces of china on their shelves. "Railways, it was. The hope of the future, he said. By the middle of the century they'd have driven all the coaches and carriers out of business. Nothing else would do but he must drag Mr. Patrick all over the country looking at engines and railways. Up to Newcastle, down to South Wales, then into Surrey, anywhere that men were experimenting with the new-fangled ways. Monsters I call them, but

73

to Mr. Henry they were miracles of power and endurance. Perhaps if Mr. Patrick had shared his father's enthusiasm, the two of them might have grown closer. But he showed no more than a boy's natural interest in mechanical things, and even that soon waned. When he began to beg off from the railway visiting and to ask if he might stay, instead, with his uncle at High Garth, Mr. Henry was disappointed and angry. He raised no objection, but it was soon after that that he started to sell his land."

Ann forgot circumspection. "To sell his *land*?" she queried, scarcely believing that she had heard aright. For this was heresy. A man did not sell his land—unless driven by necessities too shocking to contemplate.

Janet nodded, divided between triumph at a reaction so gratifying and regret for the cause of it. "I can't say as I rightly understand such matters," she confided, "but it seems that only the Court itself, with the home farm, was what they call 'settled estates'. Mr. Henry was free to sell the rest if he saw fit. Which he did. Though I still hold to it that he was wrong to sell the stands of timber that had been hundreds of years a-growing. Fair murder, that was. Hurt Mr. Patrick more than anything. More than the pictures and his mother's jewels; more than his father marrying again so soon. Yes. He sold everything that would fetch a price, did Mr. Henry, and all to buy an interest in these new railway companies."

She put the last piece of china back on its shelf and straightened up, her face austere. "You'll be thinking it ill becomes me to gossip about my betters," she said defensively, "but I was never one for making mysteries out of plain facts. Anyone can see that Mr. Patrick's gently bred, for all his shabby coat and his easy ways.

74

But when his father died there was nothing left but debts. He puts a cheerful face on it and vows that some day he'll be rich as Croesus, or whoever the king was that had his cellars stuffed with gold, but if he has to wait until the railways are finished building, dear alone knows when 'some day' will be. The Court had to be let, of course, and thankful enough he was to find a tenant for it, with the place stripped to the bone as it was. There'll be Master Philip's schooling to be thought of in a year or so. Which is why it's still make and scrape with us at the moment and every penny to be looked at twice. For let a man work all the hours the Lord gives us, yet he'll never get rich working a hill farm."

As she emptied the bowl and spread the cloths on the rosemary hedge to dry, the truth of that statement was manifest even to Ann's limited experience. Good management and unremitting toil might wrest a living from this harsh soil. It could never yield more than modest comfort. And yet already she loved the place. The keen upland air quickened her blood; the isolation, the primitive conditions, gave one the sense of belonging to a close-knit community. Not since the days of her childhood had she known this eager zest for living, this feeling that each day promised some new delight.

Not even the bad weather could depress her spirits. High Garth had been built to withstand such onslaughts. When they drew up their chairs to the wide hearth at night there was a blessed sense of security. The family was gathered within the sheltering walls of their sturdy little fortress. This was Ann's favourite hour. Philip, in the immemorial way of children, would try to defer the moment of going to bed by begging for 'just one more story.' Weary from the day's toil and pleasantly drowsy from fire-glow and hot food, the men were content to sit at ease, Will smoking his treasured clay, the others either listening to the story teller or lost in their own reflections, while the hum of Janet's spinning wheel and the soft click of the girls' knitting needles supplied a soothing accompaniment to the tale.

Philip's appetite for stories was insatiable. Thanks to Patrick's efforts during the previous winter he already knew his letters and could read a few easy words. His delight in stories, thought Ann, would surely encourage him to learn to read, and spared what time she could to satisfy his demands. It was not for several weeks that she discovered that her adult listeners had been quite as attentive as Philip. If that young man *had* a preference in stories it was for fact rather than fiction. The more exciting events of her childhood—the experiences that were commonplace to the daughters of a family that followed the drum— were soon exhausted. Frequent repetitions were demanded, but when Philip began to correct her, insisting that the exact wording be repeated each time, she decided to extend her repertoire. Fortunately Philip found her stories about London and Hertfordshire interesting in a different way. He could measure them against his own experience. She had a happy knack of enlisting his sympathy with her small triumphs and her many tribulations. He chuckled happily over her account of her own ineptitude in learning to milk. What with the stories and answering the questions that poured from the uninhibited Philip and occasionally, more shyly, from the twins, it was not long before most of the details of Miss Beverley's early life had been laid before the interested listeners at High Garth.

There came a night when Philip was sent early to

bed in punishment for having left the yard gate open when he went to visit Jigs. As a result the calves had got out, and Will, had been obliged to spend the better part of an hour in rounding up the frolicsome youngsters. Carelessness, on a farm, pronounced Patrick firmly, was criminal; especially where the safety of young stock was in question. The sinner could count himself lucky that he was not sent supperless to bed.

Ann felt quite lost without her small familiar. Philip was used to pull up his creepie beside her, lean his arms on her lap and fix her with an unwinking stare as he listened and questioned. Without that confiding warmth across her knees she felt positively bereft. Tonight even Patrick was busy, working on a model schooner that was destined for Philip's birthday gift. Opportunities for working on this masterpiece were rare, since it must be kept secret, but not even Philip would dare to creep downstairs again after being so sternly dismissed. Ann watched the strong brown fingers carefully shaping the tiny hull, their owner wholly concentrated on his task. The light was not good enough for sewing. It was almost a relief when Jenny said tentatively, "Please, Miss Ann, won't you tell us some more about Papa Fortune's town house? How many servants he keeps, indoors and out, and suchlike. Master Philip don't care for things like that, but Meg and me would fairly like to take service in London when we're old enough."

It was as well for the speaker that Janet was slightly deaf, so that the low-voiced plea did not penetrate the whirr of the spinning wheel, else it had undoubtedly brought down sharp rebuke on the girl's curly head. As it was, Ann was very willing to comply. Patiently she detailed the domestic hierarchy, beginning with the housekeeper and descending, since in a widower's

77

household there was no lady's maid to rank second, through the lower ranks of chambermaids, housemaids, laundrymaids and scullerymaids.

Jenny and Meg listened agape. And the cook was a *man*? Just fancy that, now! And a confectioner and a baker as well? Ann explained that though Mr. Fortune abhorred waste, he liked to live well. He did not employ a bailiff, since his estate was small, but there was a butler, of course, a very lofty personage, and a coachman, two footmen, a porter, a postilion and a yard boy as well as sundry grooms and two gardeners.

The girls could not imagine how so many servants could be usefully employed in securing the comfort of just one gentleman, be he never so wealthy or important, so Ann told them a little about the duties of the various maids and explained that there were a great many rooms to be kept clean, no easy task amid the smoke and dust of London.

"And parties?" queried Meg eagerly. "Does he give grand parties with all the ladies in silks and jewels?"

Ann smiled rather wryly. "He certainly entertains a good deal," she said. "But not what *you* would call parties. No ladies in fine dresses. Just gentlemen with whom he has business dealings."

Meg looked disappointed. Jenny said hopefully, "Did not you go to dress parties, Miss Ann, when you lived in Town?"

Ann laughed outright. "No, indeed! My step-papa was of the opinion that parties were a waste of time and money. The marriage market he was used to call them. And invariably added that if a female was dutiful, domesticated and well-dowered she would find a husband without having recourse to extravagant display."

"And a deal of sense in that," put in Janet dourly,

78

for though she had not heard Jenny open the subject, she had followed Ann's clear voice easily enough, if with growing concern. "I'll thank you, Miss Ann, not to go putting any fancy ideas into these silly goosecaps' heads. London, indeed! They'd be sorry enough before the month was out. Trouble with this pair, they don't know which side their bread's buttered."

Meg hung her head, abashed, but Jenny looked mulish. Ann said, "I shouldn't think they would like it at all." And to the girls, "You've no notion how horrid the older servants can be to anyone young and new-come to Town. They grumble and scold because you're clumsy, or they tease you and play tricks on you because you're green. You would get the worst of everything—the last to be served at table—an attic to sleep in—icy cold in winter, sweltering in summer. Or maybe a basement, with rats and cockroaches. Believe me, you are much more comfortably placed here."

Janet looked pleased, the girls thoughtful if not convinced. Patrick's fingers were quiet on the model boat. There was an oddly intent expression on his face, but he said nothing beyond the usual details regarding the next day's work and a courteous goodnight.

SEVEN

Next morning, however, breakfast over and morning lessons about to begin, he begged the courtesy of a few minutes private speech with Miss Beverley. Philip was bidden to study his primer by the kitchen fire and to be diligent, while his elders repaired to the sunny parlour which now was also a schoolroom.

Ann was a little surprised but in no way alarmed. After three months at High Garth she no longer feared summary dismissal. True, she still made mistakes, had occasional culinary disasters. But people were no longer kind and long-suffering about them. They laughed or grumbled, as the mood took them, and teased her unmercifully, which was infinitely preferable. As far as one faulty human being could do it, she filled her place at High Garth to a nicety, knew it, and rejoiced in her new-found confidence.

Having seated her in one of the comfortable chairs before the empty hearth, Patrick paced up and down the room a time or two before eventually coming to a halt facing her, his elbows braced upon the mantel shelf behind him his expression so stern that, for the first time, she began to feel some nervous qualms. But his voice, when at last he spoke was gentle enough, almost impersonal.

"I have to ask you one or two questions that may seem unwarrantably impertinent," he said quietly. "Will you please try to believe that only my concern for your welfare drives me to this unpleasant necessity?"

She nodded, the brown eyes fixed on him now in anxious enquiry, but he seemed indisposed to meet her gaze, turning a little aside to look out into the sunny garden which already displayed its gratitude for recent cherishing. "When you were talking to the girls last night," he began abruptly, "it was plain that you were describing the establishment of a man of wealth and position. It is scarcely within my province to enquire why, if your step-father is so well able to support you, you choose rather to earn your bread in a menial capacity with strangers. But I *must* know whether the gentleman is acquainted with your present whereabouts, and the conditions in which you are living."

The last words seemed to be wrung out of him almost against his will. Ann took her time over answering, since it seemed that the disclosure of her background of affluence had touched her employer on the raw. To a certain extent she could understand his point of view, though it was not as if he had been tricked into sheltering some runaway heiress. Or as if she, Ann Beverley, was not old enough to know her own mind.

Presently she said temperately, "Your questions are easily answered, sir. Certainly my stepfather knows my

81

present address. I wrote to inform him of it before I left Bath. And if by any chance the letter had been mislaid or gone astray, he has only to enquire of my sister. But we are not upon terms and do not correspond except upon such necessary matters, so he knows nothing of conditions here, since I myself was not fully informed when I wrote to him."

Before she could enlarge on this head, he swung round to face her, black anger in his scowl this time. "And do you imagine that he would suffer you to remain here a moment longer if he realized the truth? That you are working like some peasant in house and barn and fields? With no one to wait on you, without even the normal comforts that any gentlewoman has the right to expect?"

She waited patiently for him to finish, rather pleased than otherwise that she had understood his resentment and its cause so well, even smiling a little, despite his thunderous expression, for he had let his annoyance run away with him when he spoke of 'fields'. To be sure she had worked pretty hard in the garden, but her activities had not yet been extended to the fields, though she had high hopes of being permitted to help with the haymaking.

"If my stepfather was fully acquainted with my situation," she said calmly, "he would say that I was vastly overpaid for my services and probably read *you* a lecture on extravagance. Certainly he would not concern himself because I lacked a few luxuries."

Having long ago learned to accept her stepfather's peculiarities, her remarks were quite dispassionate. To Patrick, bitterly aware of the deficiencies of High Garth and now convinced that she regarded her present position merely as an amusing escapade with which to regale her intimates when she chose to return to her own world, the words sounded wholly flippant. He forgot the weeks of shared work and growing comradeship, the insensible lightening of his heavy burden of responsibility. He knew only that he had taken Ann Beverley at face value. He had offered her work and shelter and hospitality—simple, perhaps, but the best that he had—and all the time she had been laughing at him up her sleeve. He had even recognized the strong attraction that she could hold for him if he permitted his feelings to have their way, and had been at some pains to set a strong guard on those feelings, knowing that there could be no honourable way of pursuing intimacy with Miss Beverley. Now he wanted nothing so much as to grasp those slim shoulders hard enough to hurt, and to shake her until she was breathless and giddy, because her pretty ways had made a fool of him.

With a strong effort he controlled this desire. He said icily, "This we shall discover. If you will be so good as to furnish me with Mr. Fortune's address, I will myself write to describe to him the conditions in which you are living. I make no doubt we shall have him here to the rescue as soon as the Mail can bring him. But no! Of course not! He would scarcely condescend so far. It will be his own chaise, naturally. You will not have to endure rustic privation much longer, Miss Beverley."

At least he had had the satisfaction of startling her, even, perhaps, of frightening her a little, he thought savagely. The delicate colour was gone. The great eyes looked almost black against her pallor and her lips were trembling. He turned away abruptly, opened the bureau and drew pen and paper towards him.

"His initials?" he enquired, still icily patient.

"Plain esquire? Or does he have a title to add glamou to wealth and consequence?"

The ice was melting. That last remark was a goo deal less than dignified.

She said quietly, "I shall not tell you."

He swung round furiously. "You will *what*?"

"Not tell you," she nodded composedly. "It is n business of yours. You don't understand at all. An you are anxious only to make mischief."

There came a dangerous glint in the tawny eye "What you do while you are in my employment is ver much my business, my good girl," he reminded he grimly. "Either you obey me or you go. Now—do yo furnish me with that address—or does Will take you t catch next Wednesday's south-bound Mail?"

She stared at the harsh-set visage, utterly bewilder ed by this glimpse of a man who seemed a stranger Then she shrugged. "I suppose it was too good to last, she said wearily. "I was too happy. Very well. I'll star packing." She rose and moved slowly towards the door all the buoyancy, the gay vitality, quenched. And ther ridiculously, childishly, her hand already on the latch turned and flung at him, "And hay time starting nex week and all my plans made. You're unfair! Cruel! hate you!"

It was so blatantly honest that it penetrated Pa trick's mantle of insulted pride. Without even think ing, he crossed the floor between them in two swif strides and caught her wrist, drawing her back to th window and staring down curiously into the face tha she made no attempt to hide from him, though now after that last outburst, the tears were sliding dow her cheeks.

"Here," he said curtly, thrusting his handkerchief a

her. "Mop your eyes. Now. What *is* all this? Are you really so sorry to be leaving?"

The answer, rather naturally, was another burst of tears. But very soon, furiously despising her own weakness, she scrubbed her eyes, blew her nose, and said with dignity, if rather croakily, "I have been very happy here. Naturally I am sorry to go."

His touchy pride so fully assuaged, Patrick's world swung back into its normal orbit. He began to remember all the hard work that this slim girl had done. No spoilt society doll, playing at farming, could have gone so quietly and competently about the job.

"Yet you were prepared to do so rather than give me your stepfather's address," he pointed out.

She stared. "But naturally. That would have been to yield to blackmail." And then, since he still seemed dissatisfied, "Besides, I expect you would have painted everything in the worst possible light. And that would have given Papa Fortune a chance to crow over me. You've no idea how detestable he can be. He would dearly love to point out just where my fine high-nosed notions had got me to."

Patrick suppressed a grin at the odd mixture of high principle and childish defiance. He said gently, "I think I owe you an apology for jumping to mistaken conclusions. Perhaps if you were to tell me a little more about the gentleman—no, no, not his address," as she glanced up in swift suspicion—"I might be able to understand. Will you not sit down again?"

The story came out rather haltingly at first. The brief emotional storm had taken its toll and it was not easy to be detached about such personal matters. Moreover, having spoken so disparagingly about Papa Fortune, she was now determined to do him justice. Because he *had* his good points and she must emphasize them. He had positively doted on Mama. Nothing was too good for her. He had showered her with every luxury. It was a pity that he did not care for parties, while Mama adored them, but he had squired her about without a word of complaint and set no limit to the hospitality that she might offer in return. He had paid for the education of her daughters at a very select academy with no more demur than a query as to what females needed with all this higher education and fancy accomplishments. In his own way he had been good to them. They had resented his insistence that they should have a thorough and practical acquaintance with all the domestic arts because it took up most of their holidays and left them very little time to spend with Mama. But it had certainly stood *her* in good stead, as she did not fail to point out. And there was almost a hint of a smile with that remark. Miss Beverley was recovering her poise.

The real trouble had begun after Mama's death. Papa Fortune had always been inclined towards jealousy of the twins who, in his opinion, took up far too much of their Mama's time and affection. He had been sadly disappointed that no child had been born of his own union with Mary Beverley. Not that he had ever reproached Mama for her failure in this direction, added her daughter hurriedly.

The girls had been ten when their own father died, thirteen when Mama had re-married.

"I am bound to confess that I think she married him because of us," said Ann honestly. "For what his money could do for us. She was never very good at dealing with bills and practicalities. Neither was Papa, if it comes to that. I suppose they just muddled along contentedly together, never wondering what the future might hold, living each day as it came. And we had the happiest childhood. But after Papa died, Mama seemed only half a person. She was sweet and gentle as ever—but all the fun and sparkle was gone. And she got into dreadful muddles over money, just through not really caring. Papa Fortune is some kind of a banker, and very wealthy, I believe. But I am taking up too much of your time with my rambling tale."

He shook his head. "No. If we are to work in harmony—if you will consent to stay on after my unkindness —it is best that I should understand, so far as an outsider can."

This time it was a real smile that she gave him, and a tiny sigh of content. She had guessed herself reprieved, but it was comfortable to have the guess confirmed. She went on more easily, "We were nineteen when Mama died. It was very sudden, quite unexpected. Poor Papa Fortune was utterly stricken and dazed by his loss."

She did not speak of her own grief, but Patrick, who could remember the loss of his own much-loved mother, could well imagine the bitter desolation that she had known.

"When he began to emerge from his first shock," she went on, "it gradually became apparent that the possessive tendency he had always displayed towards Mama was being turned upon me. Barbara was newly betrothed, a very suitable match which had his full approval. Moreover she was creditably employed as a junior governess in the school where we had been educated. But I was 'just hanging about at home'. Such a gawky piece as myself, he told me, was unlikely to 'take', so I had best look to my future. He was under no legal obligation to support me, but if I would abjure the thought of matrimony, consent to take his name and to assume the charge of his household, he would see to it that as his adopted daughter I should inherit a reasonable competence at his death."

Her glance fell to his handkerchief which she was still absently pleating on her lap. "My temper is inclined to be hasty, as you are probably aware. You will readily appreciate that the discussion then became a trifle heated," she ended carefully.

He maintained a grave front in the face of a strong desire to laugh at this prim description of what he rightly guessed to have been a shattering scene. The facts, in themselves, were not amusing. For himself, he thought Mr. Fortune's suggestion iniquitous. There was a little silence, as though the girl was looking back five years and trying to recall her feelings during that momentous interview.

"I think I might have accepted the suggestion of running the household," she said thoughtfully. "I am not bookish, so such a position as Barbara's would not have done for me. Such talents as I have are domestic. I enjoy keeping a home clean and comfortable, and I like cooking. However the question did not really arise, because for no consideration would I have consented to change my name. I loved my father dearly and I am proud to be his daughter. Beverleys have always taken their share of working and fighting when it was needed. There was a Beverley at Agincourt and another at Marston Moor. And if they never achieved fame or wealth, they were respected, even honoured, by those with whom they had shared the burden of the day. If ever I marry"—she broke off and twinkled at him mischievously—"and despite Papa Fortune's gloomy prognostications I am not yet at my last prayers—I shall change my name for that of a man whom I can love and honour as I loved and honoured my father. I would never do it for money." And then as though already regretting that she had revealed so much of her heart, she said lightly, "Besides—just think how dreadful it would be to go through life greeted everywhere as 'Miss Fortune'."

He laughed. "Yes. I see. I confess I had not thought of that aspect of the case. So you parted company?"

"We did. But if you imagine that he thrust me out of doors forthwith, you do him an injustice." The voice was so cool, so impersonal, that it was difficult to assess her feelings, save by the obvious effort that she made to mask them. "Luckily, since Mama's housekeeper had just left, announcing that it was only devotion to her poor lady that had kept her there so long, I was not actually an object of charity but was able to make myself useful. And before a new one had been engaged a friend of Mama's had found me a post with *her* mama—a dear soul, but sadly crippled with rheumatism. There"—the steady voice faltered momentarily—"I was very comfortably placed for close on two years, until Mrs. Langholme died."

He could well imagine the weariness, the frustration, of this eager young creature, bound in servitude to a frail old lady, be she never so kind. Indeed, the kinder she was, the more exacting the service.

"Since then I have had a number of posts. But nowhere"—the voice was quietly intent—"have I been so happy as at High Garth. So you can imagine my distress at the thought of leaving. Perhaps that will suffice to excuse the unmerited insults that I flung at you," she ended, a little shyly.

He smiled. "Not wholly unmerited. Though I hope I am not cruel. The fault lay in my pride. I am very well aware that the hospitality of High Garth is not of the standard that I would choose to offer to a lady; and the thought that curiosity alone had brought you here and that you were just amusing yourself was enough to touch off my temper."

Ann held out hands that bore one or two burn scars and sundry other marks of toil. "Amusing myself?" she said ruefully.

"But you said you were happy here," he reminded her briskly. "And those are honourable scars that a Beverley may be proud to bear."

She laughed at that, and said that no one, Beverley or not, could be proud of the amount of work that she had done that morning. Philip would be thinking that he had been granted a holiday.

"Which reminds me that *you* have had no holiday at all since you came to us," commented Patrick. "I daresay Mr. Fortune's many minions are much better served. But it is difficult in a place like this. What can you do with a holiday, even if you are granted one?"

Ann was wondering if this was the time to drop a hint that she *would* like a holiday in September when he went on diffidently, "Would you care to come for a picnic with Philip and me? It is his birthday at the end of July, you know, and he is demanding a riding picnic. I'm not quite sure where he wants to go. Not too far, obviously, though his horsemanship is progressing apace. Since the provision of suitable food will fall upon you, it seems only fair that you should share the treat. If you would care for it," he added with meticulous politeness, and then grinned disarmingly. "Or even regard it as a treat. He'll almost certainly choose to go poking about in one of the caves with which this countryside is so liberally furnished, and that may not be at all to your taste."

"Not really," she admitted ruefully. "I was once taken to see some caves near my father's home in Somerset. They are quite famous, I believe, and everyone exclaimed over their beauty, but I, I confess, was frightened. I didn't like to feel shut in, and I was terrified that the guide's lantern would go out. But I was very young," she excused, "no older than Philip. And I expect small boys are braver."

"He's plucky enough," agreed Philip's brother, "and heedless with it. But I rather think it is the lure of gold that draws him to the caves."

Her brows lifted in enquiry.

"Legend has it that a band of Jews fleeing from York during one of the massacres that afflicted that unhappy race in mediaeval times, made their way to this part of the world and took shelter in some unidentified cavern. During the reign of King John, the story goes, which is probably why Jingling John's cave is a favourite hunting ground. Yorda's is another, though in that case I rather fancy that the mythical treasure is a Viking hoard. Whichever version you prefer, the story goes on that the refugees brought with them great treasure in gold and jewels, though why any one should suppose that the treasure is still in the caves—even if the rest of the tale is true—is more than I can well understand. However, Philip believes it implicitly, and has taken the happy notion that if only he could stumble upon the hidden gold, the fortunes of the Delvercourts would be re-established. Hence his passion for exploring the caves. But since many of them are dangerous he is not allowed to go there alone. This birthday expedition will give him a long awaited opportunity."

"Well, I shall certainly leave the exploration to the gentlemen of the party," decided Ann firmly. "I am sure the proper feminine role is the preparation of lunch for the hungry adventurers upon their return. And I feel sure we should build a fireplace and light a real fire, even if we only toast bread and bacon."

"An excellent notion," approved her employer heartily. "I begin to think I shall enjoy this expedition as much as Philip."

In this boyish mood he seemed so genial, so approachable, that perhaps it was, after all, the right time to mention Barbara's wedding, even though it was still three months away. Though how she would pacify Barbara if he made difficulties, she couldn't imagine.

Nor need she have troubled her head. Of *course* she must see her sister married he said, almost reproachfully, and then enquired with unfeigned interest as to the exact situation of Mickleford Hall and its distance from Lancaster. His solicitude made her feel quite guilty. He must not trouble himself about her travelling arrangements, she stammered. The Broughtons were to send a carriage for her, if she could get leave of absence. The road was good as far as Dent Town, and she need take very little luggage. If the season was dry and the roads good, she need be away no more than a week.

"Splendid," pronounced her employer cordially. "And pray don't make so much of the trouble you are causing. In truth there *is* no trouble about escorting you to Dent. September is our quiet season—if the weather has been kind and we are not still struggling to salvage the remains of the hay crop. But honesty compels me to admit that it is your return, rather than your departure, that concerns me. You speak of a week. I will be more generous and suggest two. But you won't succumb to the lure of Lancashire, will you, Miss Beverley? You *will* come back? For High Garth would miss you sorely."

EIGHT

It was an odd ending to an interview that had begun with a threat of summary dismissal. It sent Ann hastening back to her neglected duties with a light heart. Patrick, declaring that it was too late now to begin lessons, swept Philip off with him to watch the preparations for haytime. There were scythes to be sharpened—a skilled job this, since each blade must be replaced at exactly the right angle for its owner and the handles adjusted for his height and swing. The rakes must be examined for loose teeth and plunged into cold water to swell the wood, and then there was the hay rack to be fitted to the cart, though that would not be needed for a day or two yet.

There was still an hour before Ann need begin preparations for the mid-day meal. She started damping down a pile of linen that awaited ironing. Janet, placidly darning stockings in the sunny window, said,

"What was to do, then? Mr. Patrick seemed fair hackled about something."

During the weeks of working together, confidence and affection between the old housekeeper and the new had grown steadily. And Ann, like Janet herself, was not one for making mysteries where there was no need. She poured out the tale of the confrontation in the parlour readily enough, saying little of the encouragement bestowed upon her at its close, but elaborating on her sentiments at the prospect of dismissal.

"He'd have done it, too," nodded Janet. "I don't say he'd have sent you off with Will—that was just his temper riding him—but off you would have gone if you couldn't have explained things to his satisfaction. If he couldn't have escorted you himself he'd have got young Robert. Never one to brook defiance wasn't Master Patrick."

"It was mostly my own fault," admitted Ann. "I've got a temper, too. And *you* were cross with me last night, weren't you? I never thought of Meg and Jenny being serious about going into service in London. Goodness! If only they knew how much better off they are here."

"All young things are the same," said Janet comfortably. "You might think London was proper Paradise, pearly gates and all, the way they keep on about it. So don't *you* take on. What you said afterwards, once I'd dropped you a hint was just right. No use warning headstrong lasses of temptation and danger. They'd only think that it made it more exciting. As for Mr. Patrick you must make allowance for him. He's learned to distrust females who care only for money and novelty. One can't say Miss Errol jilted him, because the betrothal had never been puffed off in the

94

papers, but everyone knew there was an understanding between them. Only it was the Court she wanted. Far too fine and daintified for a hill farm. He's a sight better off without her—an expensive, spoiled, frivolous flirt."

In her absorption Ann sprinkled a pillow case much too liberally. This was the first time she had heard mention of romance in Mr. Delvercourt's past. She waited hopefully. Janet talked if she felt like it. Questioned, she closed up like a clam.

Presently the old woman said slowly, "I'd not have minded so much if she'd worn the willow for him. Just for a little while—for decency's sake. Maybe she wasn't to blame for admitting that she couldn't face a life of hardship such as she'd never been bred to. But she married less than a year after she found out how matters stood—*and* persuaded her husband to take a lease of the Court, so that she could queen it there as she'd always wished. Small good she got of it. The decent families held by Mr. Patrick. Naturally. There'd been Delvercourts in these parts time out of mind. Came over with Norman William did the founder of the line, so Mr. Patrick says. And a gallowsripe rogue *he* was, by all accounts. None of your noble lords but a tough captain of men-at-arms. And the name was D'Elvas. 'Twasn't for nigh on four hundred years, when the Court was just a-building, that the name and the house got mixed together and one of the family got into the history books in Queen Elizabeth's day as Jonathan Delvercourt. And the less said about *him* the better. Lucky not to end on Tower Hill. But they've mostly been good landlords and good neighbours, till Mr. Henry went railway mad. As for the Conroys— Miss Errol married a Conroy—talk about the cold shoulder! They didn't stay above three months. Then

95

they were off to Town with a lot of fine talk about the Season and parties and being buried alive in the country. They've been back a time or two since, but never for long, and tucked away up here as we are, most times we don't get to hear of their coming till they're off again. Happen it's as well."

Ann considered this judicially. "I should think such callous behaviour would have cured him of his penchant for that particular female," she offered. "You said he'd learn to distrust the type—and in any case she's married."

Janet smiled indulgently. "Easy to see you've never been in love, my lassie. His *mind* has learned to distrust her. But if he should be thrown into her company again—married or not! He'd never behave dishonourable, but she's so sweetly pretty. Small and dainty, golden curls and big blue eyes. Just like those china shepherdesses. And a confiding little way with her that made even *me* feel that I was big and strong and ought to look after her, so dear alone knows what it did to the men. It's not so easy to put that sort out of your heart, whatever common sense may say."

Ann looked rueful. "It really isn't fair, is it?" she said. "Barbie is just such another. She looks so small and feminine and helpless. If ever she's in a hobble there's always some eager gentleman ready to leap to her aid. And actually she's every bit as tough and capable as I am. As for falling in love, it's just as well I haven't. I'd have come home by weeping cross. It was plain to be seen when Mama took Barbie and me to parties. *She* was a regular honey-pot. *I* was considered sensible and conversible and given a middle-aged gentleman of sober mind for my dinner partner. It was quite unnecessary for Papa Fortune to point out that my chances in the Matrimonial Stakes were poor. I was already aware. But at least I am free to choose where I will work—and for whom!"

Brave words. But Janet guessed at the sore heart, the tear-wet pillows, when a much younger Ann had felt herself pitifully inadequate beside her pretty sister. It said a good deal for her sweetness of disposition that the experience had in no way lessened the affection in which she held that sister.

"Aye!" she admitted. "You're over tall for most men's liking, I can see that. But your face is bonnie enough, if only you'd stop wearing those caps that hide every scrap of your hair and make you look every day of thirty."

Ann laughed. "I'll discard them when I go to Mickleford to Barbie's wedding," she promised. "Maybe I'll find myself a handsome beau who'll come a-courting into Deepdale. The caps are mostly laziness you know. I wore them at first because they *did* make me look older—more like a respectable housekeeper. Then I discovered that I could abandon formal hair dressing and just plait my hair and pin it up under them, which saves *ages* in the mornings when there's so much to do."

She put the basket of linen aside for later ironing and began to mix some pastry. Janet fell silent. She was sadly disappointed, poor Janet. Almost from the first she had sensed that Miss Ann was as much out of place in a farm kitchen as Mr. Patrick himself. Her speech, her gentle ways, her fine underlinen, all gave Janet food for much speculation. Childhood has no monopoly of dreams. Like young Philip, Janet, too, dreamed of the resurgence of the Delvercourts. The prospect of her adored Mr. Patrick spending the rest of his life at High Garth—'scratting a living'—was not to be entertained. But unlike Philip she did not expect

97

miracles. Janet's dreams were founded on practical possibilities. An heiress. That was the answer. A girl with money that would bridge the gap until those dratted railways began to pay their way. And of course she would be pretty and loveable and warm-hearted. Possessed by her dream, Janet had allowed herself to weave incredible fantasies when Ann arrived. Such a romance as even her giddy-pated great-nieces would have laughed to scorn. Might not Miss Ann prove to be this much-needed heiress? To be sure it seemed odd for a young lady of fortune to work so hard and so competently. And why had she sought a position in so remote a spot? Was she, perhaps, hiding from some unwanted suitor? The victim of family persecution? It was a pity that she was not a dainty little piece like Miss Errol, the only female for whom Mr. Patrick had ever formed any sort of penchant, but that couldn't be helped.

For Janet, who had heartily disliked Lavinia Errol, even before the débâcle that had followed Mr. Henry's death, was beginning to love Ann Beverley, even though she was not the pretty puppet of her dreams. She was far better, vowed Janet fiercely. Sweet and sound as a pippin. But had she any money? To Janet's knowledgeable eye she exhibited every sign of gentle birth and an expensive education, but so did Mr. Patrick, and he had no money save what was sunk in those pesky railways.

It was a sad blow to hear, from the girl's own lips, that she had neither fortune nor prospects. In a mood of deep dejection Janet finished the last sock and announced that she was going to pull rhubarb for the pies.

Fortunately she was allowed little time for repining over her vanished dream. Two days later, after a prolonged study of the evening sky, the appearance of the young moon and the behaviour of certain animals and birds, Jim announced at supper, "Us could put scythe in tomorrow, master, if so be as you think fit."

Patrick tilted his head enquiringly towards the old man. "How long do you think it'll hold?"

"Three days for sure. Mebbe longer—even a week," opined Jim. "Might be heavy dew first thing, but it'll dry out quick enough. Be a right scorcher by noon."

All round the table faces brightened. Hay-time was hard work—but it was different. Apart from absolute essentials, ordinary routine went by the board. The women would spend most of the first day preparing food that could be carried to the fields, but after that they, too, would help in the strawing and turning, raking the hay into wind-rows and then into haycocks, ready for carrying. There would be sore hands and stiff muscles, but so long as the weather held good there would also be something of the atmosphere of a picnic.

"We'll start on the four-acre," decided Patrick. "Might as well make sure of the best. It's done well this year—heaviest crop we've had. Take a bit of drying."

Will nodded agreement. "Plenty o' work for you lasses," he grinned at the twins. "Need turning a time or two, that lot will." And the girls groaned and pretended dismay, which sorted ill with their laughing eyes.

It seemed to Ann that the moment had come to make a bid for her own share in the enterprise. "With three of us, it won't be so bad," she said, cheerfully casual.

There was silence. But at least the remark had not brought forth an immediate veto, though Will was looking dubious and Jim was slowly shaking his head.

Patrick said politely, "Every pair of hands is useful at hay-time. It is very good of you to offer your help. But it is hard work in the heat of the day, and you are not accustomed as we are. Would you not be more comfortable in the coolness of the house?"

Since his recent encounter with this single-minded damsel, he had handled her with circumspection, but in this case it served him ill. Had he said that he thought she would be better employed in the kitchen, she would have accepted the decision, albeit reluctantly, as an order. Tricked out as it was with courtesy and consideration, she felt that she might rightly contest it.

"The domestic arrangements will not suffer," she told him swiftly, casting him into some confusion since he had intended no such aspersion. "As for coolness indoors—you should have been here yesterday when we had been baking all day. I'll warrant it was hotter than any hay-field." Having demolished his argument before he had time to recover she went on more slowly, "Please let me help when I can spare the time. I promise that I will not neglect my other tasks. The thing is, you see, that my stepfather never *would* agree to my helping in the harvest fields and I did so wish to. He saw nothing demeaning in my learning to milk and churn and scrub the dairy shelves, but he would not have me, as he phrased it, 'hob-nobbing with common labourers'. But here it's different." For the first time she sounded a little shy. "Here we're—a kind of family, aren't we? So—please let me do my share."

Patrick admitted defeat. It was plain that Will and Jim who might have supported him, had been disarmed by the innocent compliment. And when Janet, too, went over to the enemy, there was no more to be said. "She'll have an hour or two to spare, with no

100

lessons to see to," pronounced Janet, "and that'll be plenty for a start. Don't let her do too much, Mr. Patrick. No use knocking yourself up, Miss Ann, and no one with the time to wait on a sick room. What's more you'll need something cooler than that gown you're wearing, *and* a sun-bonnet. Those caps of yours won't do. Something to shade your face and the back of your neck is what's needed. I daresay I can find one that will serve."

Ann, feeling about seven years old as everyone nodded endorsement of Janet's remarks, accepted the offer gratefully and, on the plea of putting Philip to bed, quietly effaced herself before anyone could think of further advice or restrictions. Patrick decided gloomily that two conniving females in one household was one more than an ordinary man could manage. Such help as Miss Beverley might give would be more than offset by the added responsibility of seeing that she didn't overdo things. He hadn't the heart to depress her eagerness, but she was not of the same sturdy breed as the twins and the work would be too hard for her.

Also, in his inmost thoughts, he admitted to another reason for his reluctance to see her working in the fields. It was an absurd reason—quite out of place in a practical hard-working farmer. It was just that he did not want to see that delicate skin exposed to the ravages of wind and sun. Though he was at some pains to conceal it, Miss Beverley's lovely purity of colouring gave him considerable pleasure. The same sort of artistic satisfaction, he assured himself, that he derived from the contemplation of beauty in any form. It would be a pity to see that perfection marred. But wilful women would have their way. He hoped that Janet's sun-bonnet would provide adequate protection, and recalled that Miss Beverley's charming complexion had apparently taken no hurt from the fierce Iberian sunshine, shrugged philosophically, and turned his thoughts to more profitable channels.

The next day's weather actually improved upon Jim's prophecy, since there was no heavy dew to delay the start. Moreover there was a pleasant breeze which, said Will cheerfully, would dry the stuff out in no time at all. The twins, carrying down well-filled baskets to the workers at noon, came back to report good progress. More than half the field was down already. As soon as they had eaten their own dinners and washed the pots, they were to go back and start strawing.

Ann would dearly have loved to go with them, but Janet was adamant. It was the hottest part of the day. The breeze had dropped, though it would freshen again towards evening, and strawing the fresh-cut grass was heavy work. Time enough to try out her 'prentice hand when it had dried out a bit. Better to get the milking over with a bit earlier than usual, then they could take the afternoon drinkings down to the field and stay on to help.

However she was pleased to approve the well-worn pink dimity that the girl proposed to wear, since it was long sleeved and high to the throat, thus affording protection from the sun, and hurried off to her own room to find a sun-bonnet.

She came back with a bonnet of dark brown linen perched on her hand, declaring that she hadn't liked it when she bought it. "It's a dowie sort of colour," she complained, "but it was the only one that Bridie had left the last time she was up. And it's the only one that's like to fit *you*," she added, eying the thick fair plaits that hung to the girl's waist.

While Ann stripped off her grey house gown and hurried into the pink dimity, Janet proceeded to explain about Bridie. "For you'll be seeing her, like as not, before next month's out. She's a pedlar woman. Makes her way through the dales, selling her wares and buying knitted goods to sell in Kendal market. And as decent a body as ever stepped. An Irish girl she was, that married a Romany—if marriage you can call it, by their heathenish rites. Her husband was killed in a knife fight and she was left with this daughter that grew up to marry Will."

Ann turned and stared. She had never thought of Will as anything but a bachelor.

"Only the girl was wild as a moor pony," Janet went on, "neither to hold nor bind. Scarce a year wed and she was off with a soldier. That bonnet'll never go over that quantity of hair," she put in, as Ann pinned up the thick coils. "You'll have to dress it different."

The abrupt change of subject made Ann start, so absorbedly had she been listening to the tale. "Yes. Go on," she said, pulling the pins out of her hair. "What happened?"

"Why—nothing. Only that it's Will that Bridie clings to, not her own flesh and blood. Always a good flannel shirt put aside for him from her pack to keep him warm in the bitter winters. You'll have to get her to tell your fortune. Lot o' nonsense I daresay, but it's queer how often she hits off the truth. Claims she has the sight, does Bridie, and her the seventh child of a seventh child. But Mr. Patrick says it's just a mixture of shrewdness and commonsense. Did you never think to have your hair cut, Miss Ann?"

But Ann, struggling to force the bonnet over the silver-fair plaits, said that her father had been proud of her luxuriant mane and had begged her never to

103

succumb to the temptation of a fashionable crop.

"Well there's no way it'll go under that bonnet. Here. Let me try."

A search in a neatly kept sewing basket produced a knot of tape. She bound a length firmly round the end of each plait and looped them up to tie again at the nape. Because of their thickness the plaits stuck out sideways with an endearingly quaint effect, but at least the bonnet would now go on.

Satisfied that the fair skin was now protected from the sun, Janet did not stop to study the effect of her efforts. Neither did Ann, much too impatient to be on her way, save for a passing thought that she must look slightly ridiculous. She tied the bonnet strings under her chin, picked up the baskets that she had packed with such care, and with Janet carrying the jugs, set off for the four-acre meadow.

Only as the girl set down the baskets to open the gate did Janet glance at the eager face framed in the dark brown bonnet and suddenly wonder if she had done wisely. But who could have guessed that a childish hair style and a plain brown bonnet could have effected such a transformation? Perhaps the soft rose of the dress, so different from the sober hues that the girl usually affected, was partly responsible. Janet was not given to flights of romantic fancy, but she could clearly recall a picture in one of Mr. Patrick's nursery picture books. The tale was all about a lost princess masquerading as a goose girl. Save that she carried baskets instead of herding geese, Miss Beverley might have posed for that self-same picture.

NINE

What Patrick thought of this sudden transformation in the appearance of his staid young housekeeper was not immediately apparent. Since early manhood he had learned to exercise rigid self control in the face of a series of disconcerting discoveries. The exercise served him well now, and the check in the smooth rhythm of his scythe passed unnoticed in the general focussing of interest on the contents of the baskets.

No one thought it odd that he should move steadily on to the end of his swathe before joining the others, or that he should sit a little apart, slightly withdrawn from the eager chatter of the twins. Presently he was able to permit his glance to rest casually upon that slender rose-clad figure, to mark with quiet satisfaction her handling of the twins. They were a little above themselves, exclaiming over her changed appearance with a freedom that might so easily have become displeasing. Yet her innate dignity, her gentle manner, kept them from going beyond the line without quelling their exuberance too harshly.

Patrick knew very well that he, too, had gone beyond the line. The transition from a warm liking, half amused, half respectful, to a love that he already recognized as hopeless, had happened in the blink of an eye. That it was bound to create painful problems and could only end in self denial and bitter loss, he was very well aware. But for the moment he was content to savour present happiness.

If he was quieter than usual over supper that night, so were they all, drowsy from the long hours of toil and the heavy sweet scent of the new-mown hay, even Philip willing for once to go early to bed. Only Janet thought it strange, not to say foolish, that Master Patrick should choose tonight of all nights to stroll out after supper with a casual recommendation tossed over his shoulder that no one should wait up for him. With the prospect of unremitting labour while the weather held, he should have sought his bed like the others. Worried about money, she surmised sadly, and lay wondering where it might be possible to make further economies until she drifted into well-earned slumber.

Despite his physical weariness, Patrick was urgent to be away from the farm with its windows like watching eyes, the gleam of a candle still showing from Ann's room where the girl was patiently brushing out and re-braiding the silky masses of her hair. He strode down the farm track to the lane. This was high summer when the night sky was never really dark. The young moon showed only faintly against its tender blue. One bright star pricked out from a drifting veil of rosy, feathery clouds. But Patrick was in no mood to appreciate the beauties of nature. He had borne himself with dignity and reticence in the face of a

106

shattering discovery. Now he craved only solitude in which to come to grips with his dilemma.

He walked on down the lane, which lay in deep shadow between its high banks, until he came to a spot much beloved by Philip, where a beck cast itself over a ledge in impetuous cascade. Here he paused and leaned his weary body against a convenient tree, insensibly soothed by the water noises and the comforting dusk.

Here was the very situation that he had dimly foreseen and feared. Love had grown within him, credibly disguised as liking, until he was suddenly shocked into recognition by the sight of a girl's face framed in a serviceable brown bonnet. He permitted himself a brief recollection of that moment; the eager anticipation in the big brown eyes; the soft sheen on the delicate skin that he longed to touch and kiss. After their recent talk he could not help knowing that the cards were stacked in his favour. She was lonely— desperately lonely. She loved High Garth and her life there. She was fond of Janet and the girls and he thought she liked and trusted *him*. If he wooed her, as instinct bade, could he not teach her to love him in return? Then they could marry and live contentedly at High Garth. Let the world go by.

The even ripple of the beck was broken as some small creature swam across. A hunting owl drifted over-head. Patrick sighed. Lavinia Errol had shown him that life was not so simple as a man might think. To be sure, Ann was no Miss Errol. But Lavinia had made it very plain that no woman of breeding could endure the hardships of a hill farm. Maybe he *could* coax Ann into believing the world and its comforts well lost for love. But was it fair to do so? Lavinia's lesson had cut deep. If a man could not lap his wife in luxury, then he should not marry. Patrick dismissed the wistful dream of a woman who would be more than willing to share his fortunes and bear his children—so that she and they were his.

With marriage ruled out of court, what was best to be done? *He* could not leave the farm, and Ann obviously didn't wish to do so. Yet he did not feel he could long endure their close association without betraying himself. If that happened he would be forced to send her away—though probably she would take the initiative herself. And in the midst of his anxious deliberations he grinned wryly. At least he would not give her cause to set about him with a candlestick!

Perhaps when she went off to her sister's wedding she would recognize more clearly the stark nature of her present existence and would decide against returning. She might even meet some eligible gentleman who would wish to marry her. If he truly loved her, he ought to wish for something of the sort. The difficulty was that he found it impossible to visualize any imaginary suitor who could be worthy of his beloved Ann, though he found no difficulty at all in picturing the various means of dealing with this paragon if he should ever appear in the flesh.

The activities of the next few days gave him little time for romantic yearnings. He took the risk of cutting the third meadow, leaving Jim and the girls to finish leading the first. After that it was a race between the workers and the weather. The fifth morning was grey and sultry. The sun was veiled; the little breeze had died. They were working in the last field, the furthest from the house, and here the growth was uneven because of the slope of the land. Half of it was dry enough for leading, but the thicker stuff in the bottoms still showed greenish. They worked on steadily, opening up the damp windrows, raking up the rest ready for leading, Philip proudly taking charge of Maggy, who knew a good deal more about the business than he did.

The day became oppressively hot. They had agreed that they would not stop for a meal but would work straight through in an effort to beat the threatened storm, but Ann, going up to the house with the second load, brought back jars of nettle beer and a basket filled with generous hunks of jam pastry. She was greeted with acclaim. The sharp cool drink was very refreshing and the pasties vanished with surprising speed.

"That was a good notion," nodded Patrick approvingly. "We'll work the better for it."

A rumble of distant thunder added point to the reminder. The workers returned to their tasks, Ann, flushed with gratification, hastily gathered up the debris of the impromptu lunch and stowed it under the hedge before joining them.

It was three o'clock before they finished the last load and Philip, as the youngest, rode triumphantly back to the laithe on top of the swaying, bumping vehicle. By that time the thunder was close and an occasional vicious stab of lightning set the twins squealing hysterically, but blessedly the rain still held off, and they had stowed the last rakings safely on the baulks before the first heavy drops fell. The twins, who had been enviously watching Philip indulging in the age-old pastime of jumping from the baulks into the soft hay piled in the moo, and regretting that petticoats and advancing years prevented them from emulating his exploits, went scuttering up to the house, there to be scolded by Janet for leaving Miss Ann to start the milking alone.

But even Janet's scolding was half-hearted. No one could be out of humour on such a joyous day. The hay crop was the mainstay of the farm's economy, and this year they had got in a bumper crop in prime condition. It was a very cheerful and extremely hungry party that presently gathered in the big kitchen. Janet had cooked supper while Ann was busy in the dairy, and in honour of the occasion she had cut into the last ham—there would be no more till November brought pig killing—and had heaped their plates with the pink-brown sizzling slices, helped out by potatoes baked in the embers. With rhubarb pie to follow, Patrick vowed it was a feast fit for a king, and when she triumphantly brought out a jug of cream to go with the pie there were exclamations of delight, for this was a rare treat. But then, as she pointed out, there had been no time *this* week for butter making.

Will wanted to know if there was any more of 'that there nettle beer' and Ann, bringing out the last jug, told how she had learned to make it from the farmer's wife on Papa Fortune's Hertfordshire estate, who swore by it as a specific for cooling the blood. Will did not seem to be greatly concerned with *this* property of the beverage, but earnestly suggested that it would be a good thing if miss made a lot more of it next year, even going so far as to volunteer to cut the nettles for her, since the task must involve blistered fingers.

Ann, tired but happy, basked contentedly in the thought that her presence at next year's hay time was taken for granted, never dreaming that her employer, placidly supping his nettle beer, was wondering how much longer he could maintain the facade of easy camaraderie.

The girl had pulled off her sun-bonnet, but in the press of work to be done there had been no time to change her gown or dress her hair. With the fat plaits dangling on her shoulders, a few loose tendrils waving about her temples and nape, a few tiny freckles powdering her nose, she looked young and carefree and happy, and Patrick wanted nothing so much as to take her in his arms and caress the petal skin with gentle lips, freckles and all, before he kissed the innocent mouth.

Will, commenting approvingly on the rain, which was now "fair siling down" and the beneficial effects that this would have on the turnips and a possible second growth of "fog" in the fresh cut meadows, diverted his thoughts to more practical matters. They began to plan the work of the coming week.

TEN

The end of hay time might make life a little less strenuous for the men folk but it ushered in a busy season in kitchen and dairy. Berries and currants were ripening fast and Ann was eager to make all the jams and pickles that she could, not only from the produce of the old garden, but from the abundance of wild fruits—bilberries, crab-apples and later, she hoped, blackberries. Cheese making had begun, too. She was busy from dawn till supper time, but she was young and strong and the work offered plenty of variety, so she sang as she worked and bloomed visibly. Life was good. No thoughts of ill-starved romance clouded her enjoyment.

Her one small remaining anxiety was Philip's education. This progressed rather erratically. Hay time had meant a break of a whole week, and a small boy was naturally reluctant to settle down to steady routine again. He had made excellent progress in reading and his penmanship was fair. His general knowledge was superior, for he had an enquiring mind and a retentive memory. But arithmetic he detested. They were still struggling with the two times table, and though he could count and add pretty accurately, subtraction remained a mystery. One, moreover, which he had no desire to solve. He became adept at the gentle art of creating a diversion whenever the hated sum book came out.

Why, he enquired one morning, did Miss Beverley teach him to make figures which were different from the ones on the kitchen clock? Encouraged by this sign of interest, Ann spent some ten minutes in explaining about Roman numerals and how complicated they became when you wanted to write large numbers. Philip, who could tell the time pretty well when it suited his purpose, marked with delight that both hands of the clock were approaching the figure eleven, which would signal his release. When she showed signs of reverting to the sum book, he said innocently, "Then if there are different ways of counting, why don't you teach me to count 'Yan, tan, tethera', like Jim does when he's counting his sheep? That's the Yorkshire way."

"Because when you go to school, all the other boys would laugh at you," said Ann patiently. "You wouldn't like that, would you?"

"And because if I were to spank you, my lad, it would hurt just as much if I counted yan, tan, tethera as if I said one, two, three," said a quiet voice behind her, "and you wouldn't like that, either."

Patrick had come in through the dairy entry, kicking off his muddy boots to avoid trailing the dirt into the kitchen, so that they had not heard him. Ann wondered how long he had been standing there. Philip flushed scarlet and ducked his head.

113

"I had thought to ask you if this young rapscallion might have a holiday from lessons on Friday, which is his birthday," Patrick went on sternly. "And I find him deliberately idling. Yan, tan, tethera, indeed! It might be better if he foregoes holidays until he has learned to mind his book, if he is not to grow up an ignorant young savage with no better prospect in life than counting sheep."

At this dreadful threat Philip's eyes filled with tears, though he manfully closed his lips on the sob that tried to escape. Ann felt the rebuke quite as much as her pupil, even if she did not show her discomfort so plainly. But the downcast eyes, the underlip caught in white teeth, spoke plainly enough to the perceptive eyes of love. Patrick cursed his clumsiness. He had meant only to help her, to strengthen her hand. Instead he had distressed her. How best to mend matters?

He dropped a hand on Philip's shoulder and said gruffly, "Be off with you, idle-bones. I'll try if I can coax Miss Beverley to come with us on Friday. And after supper tonight, we'll see how you acquit yourself with the twice times."

His mind relieved of its prime anxiety, Philip gathered up his slate and pencil and fled. Patrick turned to the silent girl. "Young horror, isn't he?" he said cheerfully. "I don't know how you keep your patience. But give him his due, he's an ingenious little devil. Last year—before you came—it was putting off bedtime. You've no notion of the excuses he devised. His milk was too hot—or too cold; he hadn't said his prayers; the moonlight would keep him awake; the string of his nightshirt was in a knot and he couldn't undo it; the milk had made him thirsty and he wanted

114

a drink of water—no end to it. *You* seem to manage much better. I wish you will teach me the trick of it before you desert us in September."

Ann revived swiftly to this skilled handling. The meek apologies dried on her lips. "Because I tell him stories if he comes right away," she confessed, laughing. "I'm not sure whether it's blackmail or bribery—but it's not a very moral approach."

Patrick laughed too. "It works—that's the main thing. I've been meaning to compliment you on the improvement in him. He is happier and busier and better mannered. It has made a vast difference to me, having the care of him taken off my hands. Is he making reasonable progress in his studies?"

"Except for arithmetic," agreed Ann, shaking her head, but no longer feeling crushed by her own deficiencies.

"Yan, tan, tethera?" teased Patrick. "For myself I always had a soft spot for 'Yan-a-bomfit' and the beautiful finality of 'Gigit', though I never ventured to tease my tutor with them. But he *is* only six, after all. Which reminds me, what about this picnic? Can you manage it? You know I sometimes wonder how we did before you came. Certainly we were never so comfortable or so well fed. I have good cause to call down blessings on a certain brass candlestick!"

Such praise, when she had looked for reprimand, put Ann in a glow of happiness. She blushed rosily and stammered confused thanks, her mind already busy with plans for a picnic lunch that should rival Mrs. Hartley's. Patrick said that Bob Alder was very willing to lend Donna for her to ride. He himself would ride Maggy and Philip had Jigs. It remained only to discover Philip's wishes as to the selected spot.

But Philip, approached on this head after supper,

had a surprise for them. He had acquitted himself very creditably with the two times, having spent the hour before supper in rhythmic recitation, and his face shone with the confidence of recent achievement as he said, "I want to go to the Court. It's not so *very* far if we cut across by Hollin Bush. Is it, Will?"

"It's a mighty long way for Jigs," said Will uncomfortably. So that was why the child had been so uncommon persistent in his enquiries as to the exact direction of the Court. Will rather wished that he had not been so helpful with his replies.

Patrick looked dubious. "It *could* be done," he admitted, "if we made an early start. But why the Court, brat? There's nothing to do there. And to make no bones about it, I'd as soon not picnic on land that was once ours. Wouldn't you rather go exploring in Kingsdale?"

Philip's chin jutted obstinately. "No. Not this time. Because I want to see if my acorns are growing."

Even Patrick looked blank at this. Seeing their mystification, Philip elaborated.

"Papa had lots of trees cut down. So Sturdy said we must plant some more. And he gave me a whole bag of acorns."

Since Sturdy was the lodge-keeper at the Court, the matter was now plain, and though Patrick viewed with distaste the prospect of re-visiting his childhood home in what seemed to him a somewhat clandestine manner, he raised no further objection. There were not many treats in Philip's life. He would not spoil this one by showing his own reluctance.

The weather, at any rate, chose to favour the picnic, and Jim promised them that there would be no rain to spoil their pleasure. They set out early. The horses would have to be rested in the heat of the day, and,

116

as usual, there were several places where they would have to walk. Patrick said little, but Philip made up for it. He was filled with the glory of being seven, only slightly tarnished by the fact that he had been obliged to leave his birthday gifts behind, all save the woollen cap presented by Meg and Jenny. This he had insisted on wearing, though it would have been difficult to imagine a more unsuitable head-gear for a scorching July day. He had also failed in a spirited attempt to convince his brother that there would be plenty of space for the model schooner in one of the saddle bags, and that the little lake at the Court was just the place for a ceremonial launching. It seemed impossible to convince the child that he could no longer come and go as he pleased in his former home.

This brief set-back was promptly forgotten once he was in the saddle. He was soon chattering away as gaily as ever, drawing Ann's attention to such features of interest as appealed to a small boy. These ranged from the bleached skull of a rabbit to a derelict cottage where Will had told him that you might find an owl's nest. Scenery held no attraction for him, but it was different with his elders. They were coming now to a softer, richer country. Ann might have succumbed to the wild magic of Deepdale's high fells, and because they were her first love they would always have a special place in her heart. But the Dee valley in high summer had beauty of a different kind, a gentle maturity that held nothing of complacence. These lush pastures, too, would endure the savage onslaught of winter at high altitudes, but this was their smiling time. They lay open, fertile, welcoming; and every curl of the track presented new vistas of changing loveliness. Ann, suddenly aware of the exhilaration of holiday, of new sights and scents, straightened in the saddle and sniffed the mingled odours of gorse blossom and hay and river with deep appreciation.

With the decision to ride to the Court rather than into Kingsdale, the idea of a camp fire had been abandoned. Fortunately it had never reached Philip's ears! Perhaps next time, thought Ann cheerfully, in the confident assumption that she would be there to make one of the party. Patrick suggested that they should lunch by the river, where wide shelves of sun-baked rock offered themselves as seats and tables. It was a delightful spot, with trees sufficient to give a shade for the horses and the song of the river to provide an accompaniment to idle talk.

A small boy and a shallow stream need no entertainment from grown-ups. Philip was never out of sight. He wandered back to them once or twice, to show a pebble, "all stripey like a peppermint humbug", to report the presence of a trout, "at least *that* long" under a big rock, and to renew his supply of eatables, but to all intents and purposes they might as well have been alone. Ann, busy with the food, was quite unconscious of self, and Patrick, lulled by the beauty of the day, allowed himself to forget everything but the pleasure of watching her, beneath lids lowered, presumably, against the brilliant sunlight. He wished, idly, that she had been wearing the old pink dress. In that she had seemed young and vulnerable—almost attainable. Today's riding dress, though plain enough, gave her an elegance that put her beyond his touch. But at least for today she was all his. He watched with tender amusement as she set out the carefully prepared feast.

Because it *was* a feast, she had roasted a chicken, cunningly seasoned with rosemary and carefully prepared for picnic eating. She had baked little white bread cakes to go with it, crusty outside and soft within, getting up at four o'clock so that they should be baked in time and eaten in their first perfection. Luckily in all the birthday excitement no one had commented on the smell of fresh-baked bread that pervaded the kitchen. And greatly daring, she had brought a pot of butter mixed with chopped thyme and parsley to spread on the bread, though knowing the dubious eye with which men folk always regarded strange foods, she had taken the precaution of bringing one of plain butter as well. It had been her first action, once the picnic place was chosen, to set these, and one or two other items to cool in the stream. Philip surveyed the portion that his brother had accepted and wanted to know what had turned the butter green, but seeing Patrick eat it with obvious relish was persuaded to try one himself, after extracting a promise that he need not finish it if he didn't like it. He took a very tentative bite and made no comment, but Ann noticed that he took two more pieces, well laden with slices of chicken, before retreating to his chosen vantage point, a rock in midstream that could only be reached with the help of three rather wobbly stepping stones.

"This bread is absolutely delicious," said Patrick suddenly. "No, not the herb butter, though that's good, too. The bread itself. Did you make it?"

Ann nodded, pleased.

"And what time did *you* get up this morning?" demanded her employer acutely.

She grinned, and told him. "But it was for Philip's birthday," she pleaded excusingly, seeing his brows draw together.

It served. His anger melted, though he did his best to sound severe as he told her, "*You* are a thoughtless headstrong chit! You'll be dying on my hands before I

119

get you home tonight. Up at four—and then riding all day. Never heard of anything so ridiculous."

Ann stared at him solemnly, made a gallant attempt to look guilt-stricken and penitent, and giggled.

The mobile brows lifted enquiringly.

"I was just remembering some of our childhood adventures," she explained. "I'm no sheltered flower, you know. I was brought up to early rising—even to riding all night at times, with food and sleep snatched where they could be got."

"That's as maybe. But while you are in my charge you'll take no such foolish risks with your health," he returned firmly. "What's more, you will rest for an hour now, before we set out again."

She protested that she was not in the least tired but he paid no heed, arranging an empty saddle bag and his discarded jacket to make a pillow for her and cutting a couple of armloads of bracken to soften the contours of the unyielding rock. "So seasoned a campaigner should be able to sleep on that," he told her. "Try to catch up on some sleep. Philip and I will investigate the possibilities of that trout, but we'll not go out of earshot."

She closed her eyes obediently, half pleased by his concern, half resentful of his masterful ways. The makeshift couch was surprisingly comfortable, the murmur of voices, an occasional shriek of excitement from Philip, mingled with the stream noises to provide reassurance. Before she had done wondering how long she must lie passive before she dare get up and join in the fun, she was asleep.

Perhaps she was not quite the seasoned campaigner that she had pretended, but she did possess one attribute that most soldiers eventually acquire. However deep her sleep, she usually awoke to immediate awareness of her situation. So it was on this occasion. She lay still for a moment, savouring the luxury of sun-soaked idleness and wondering vaguely how long she had slept. She could still hear the murmur of Patrick's voice, though he was speaking very softly, doubtless out of consideration for her supposedly sleeping self. What a beautiful speaking voice he had, she thought dreamily. Softened and deepened as it was now, a voice to entrance the sense.

Ann heard him say, "But today at least I may keep. Today you are mine. All my life I shall remember the curve of your cheek pressed against my old jacket, the softness of your mouth, relaxed in sleep, and the lovely shape of your small scarred hands against the green of the bracken."

There was an odd thundering in her ears. Her heart was behaving in a most peculiar way. It seemed to be beating madly somewhere in her throat till she felt as if she must suffocate. But she could not *really* have heard those words? For once dreams must have carried over into waking.

Startled, half unwilling, she opened her eyes. Patrick was leaning against a birch tree, one arm crooked round a convenient branch. On his face, half hidden in the tree's dappled shade, she glimpsed for a moment such an expression of adoring tenderness that involuntarily she gasped and blinked in sheer disbelief. It was only for an instant. But when she opened her eyes again he was smiling down at her in perfectly friendly fashion and saying apologetically, "Did I startle you? I came to see if you were awake. Philip has been building a dam, and he demands your presence at the great moment when he releases the pent-up waters."

Philip's voice calling from the river completed the return to normality. Ann accepted the hand that was

121

offered to help her to her feet and scrambled down to the bed of the stream, still a little uncertain as to whether or no she had dreamed the whole. Watching Philip as he jumped triumphantly on the erection of turves and stones—to the considerable detriment of his clothes—she put aside the warm intimacy of those moments of waking; carefully, as one would place in quietness and safety, some small feathered creature that had fluttered unaware within one's grasp. Later— tonight perhaps—she would permit herself to remember.

ELEVEN

Loitering so long by the river, they must waste no more time, announced Patrick, or they would be late for the birthday spread that Janet had promised to prepare against their return. But the horses were well rested and very willing and they made good speed along a much-used bridle track. Ann was quite thankful for Donna's playful ways, since they demanded all her attention. Patrick was quiet, but perhaps that was the hurt of returning as an alien to his lost home. Philip was quiet too, but Ann had no hesitation in ascribing this to a surfeit of jelly and fruit pie. Certainly he sprang to eager life when they overtook a red-headed lad somewhat older than himself, jogging along placidly on a fat cob.

"Sam! Sam!" he cried joyously, ranging alongside. "It's my birthday, and we've come to see you. And this is my very own pony."

"Sam Sturdy," explained Patrick, as the lad

grinned at them bashfully. "Anyone at home at the Court, Sam?"

The lad rubbed his nose. "Well—yes and no, sir," he said doubtfully. "They bin back best part of a week, but never to 'ome much. Happen Sir Stephen's somewhere about place, but 'er ladyship drove off into Kendal just afore I set out. Spankin' new carriage and all."

Ann could not help seeing the tightening of the knuckles as Patrick's brown fingers clenched on Maggy's rein, but his voice was careless enough as he said, "Miss Beverley and I are scarcely dressed for an afternoon call. Do you think your father would permit you to accompany Philip on his explorations?"

"Aye, sir," said Sam with enthusiasm. "'e'll be right pleased to see't lile master. An' me mum'll give us some parkin and buttermilk so's us'll not go 'ungry."

Philip accepting this suggestion with the mien of one who has not eaten for several days, the party split up. "No more than an hour," cautioned Patrick. "Meet us at the Lodge gate at half past three. Miss Beverley and I will ride on a little way."

Nevertheless he hesitated noticeably before he said, "Are you interested in old houses, Miss Beverley? Would you like to see the outside of the Court? Since my father cut down the trees, one gets an excellent view from the road, though I regret that it is not in my power to show you over the house itself."

What could she do but express polite compliance? Even though she was perfectly sure that her companion had no least desire to gaze at the exterior of his former home.

They rode on in silence. The lane curved in a wide sweep round the west wing of the old house, following a boundary wall of dressed stone that had mellowed over the years to a pleasing blend of honey-gold and grey. Their first glimpse of the house was through a narrow Gothic arch, where a wrought-iron gate revealed smooth green turf stretching unbroken to terraces 'set with stone urns that held a glowing burden of bloom.

"There's actually a ha-ha wall between us and the house," explained Patrick, his voice dispassionate as though he were some paid guide. "This was used to be part of the park in my grandfather's day, and there was a small herd of deer that *would* raid the gardens—or so my grandmama told me. Hence the ha-ha."

They rode on. Impossible to stop and stare as she would have liked to do had she been alone. For the Court was lovely. Just the kind of house that she liked, neither vast nor fashionably elegant. A solid family house that had grown with the passing of the years, as succeeding generations needed more rooms, or just wished to cut a dash. Because they had built in local stone and with due consideration for the northern climate, the result was a harmonious blend of architectural styles which fitted admirably into its background of green pasture and rolling fell. If houses could be said to have personalities, thought Ann, this one was friendly. Comical, too. It bore itself with dignity, as was only seemly in view of the impressive armorial bearings carved over the main door, but it was not above a gentle jest. The windows seemed to twinkle in greeting, and several of them were oddly shaped and placed. There was a small round one that especially intrigued her, but she did not like to question her taciturn escort. Loving High Garth as she did, taking pleasure in enhancing its appearance and defending it loyally against criticism, she realized in part what it must have meant to Patrick to give up the home of his boyhood, the home to which, no doubt, he had confidently expected to bring his bride.

"A pity I cannot show you the fountain," said the polite automaton at her side. "It looks very pretty in the sunshine. But the water gardens and the lake that Philip spoke of—a very miniature affair—are behind the house, and the lane is private."

And you, she thought sympathetically, would not trespass by so much as an inch, and said quietly, "It is very lovely. The whole valley is beautiful. Have we time to ride on as far as the river? The Rawthey, isn't it?"

She had snatched at the first excuse that came to mind in order to draw him away from a sight that could only be painful, and he followed her lead very willingly, speaking in a much more natural way of boyhood fishing exploits in that same river. But she soon had cause to regret her impulsive suggestion. Down the road at a gentle trot came a shiningly new barouche drawn by two splendid match bays. The top was folded back so that an admiring public might gaze upon its solitary occupant, who had thus been obliged to put up a charming parasol to protect her complexion. The entire turnout would have looked very much more at home in Hyde Park.

It scarcely needed the slight check in Patrick's voice, the sudden stiffening that caused the patient Maggy to twitch her ears nervously, to advise Ann of the newcomer's identity. Even as realization dawned there was a tiny scream of joyous surprise. The parasol was cast aside, the horses halted.

"Patrick! Oh! How delightful! And to think that I should be from home the very first time that you chose to visit me! *So* fortunate that I decided not to go as far as Kendal after all. I meant to, you know, to try out

126

my new pair. Are they not splendid creatures? Stephen gave them to me so that I can lionize in the Park." There was a dimple and a tiny gurgle of laughter for this. "So I thought I would visit my dear Mary—Mary Rushton, you know. And then if we did not run slap into her in Sedbergh, and *she* was going to visit some elderly cousins—or were they aunts? Anyway, equally fusty I daresay. So what with Joe, there"—the delightful smile flickered over the coachman but left him visibly unmoved—"grumbling about taking the horses out in this heat, and knowing that provincial shops are vastly inferior to London ones, I thought I might just as well come home again. What could have been better judged. Were you meaning to ride as far as Kendal seeking me?"

The flood of easy babble swept on. Ann felt a quite unaccountable depression. Janet had not over-praised the young chatelaine of the Court. She was indeed beautiful. And if her blue muslin gown was rather elaborate for carriage wear, it looked cool and dainty and exactly matched the big appealing eyes. Even her voice was delightful, so that it really didn't matter that she spoke nothing more than the merest commonplaces. And no doubt her hands were white and well-tended beneath her blue kid gloves. Ann bit her lip, thankful that she, too, was wearing gloves, though why she must start worrying her head over hands and gloves at this juncture, she really couldn't imagine.

Patrick succeeded at last in stemming the flow of chit-chat, explaining about Philip's birthday. "We had not the intention of calling at the Court," he said quietly, "were not even aware that you were in residence. But pray permit me to present Miss Beverley."

At once Lady Conroy was all charming apology. Miss Beverley must forgive her. Such an old friend as

Patrick—she feared she had forgotten her manners. How delightful to find a *new* friend in this barbarous countryside. Miss Beverley must come up to the Court where she might repose herself and enjoy a cool drink while they became acquainted. She did not actually add, "And brush the dust off your habit and set your hair to rights," but she looked it, sweeping Ann with an appraising glance and promptly dismissing her as negligible.

Ann glanced questioningly at Patrick. She had no least desire to improve her acquaintance with Lady Conroy. That cool elegance made her feel grubby and homespun, and the faint air of patronage set up all her prickles. But she did not know whether Patrick wished to go or to stay.

He said smoothly, "You are very kind, Lavinia, but I fear that I must deny Miss Beverley that pleasure. Philip will be waiting for us and we have still a long ride ahead."

Neither big blue eyes nor pretty coaxing served to persuade him. Ann, tactfully silent, was permitted to glimpse another aspect of the spoiled beauty. Even this small rebuff brought a petulant droop to the beautiful mouth, a waspish note to the soft voice. Finally, admitting defeat, she tossed her head—a trick that should have been spanked out of her in childhood, decided Ann with professional interest—and said spitefully, "Very well. Go then. Doubtless you will find better entertainment than I can offer."

The pair rode on towards the river, the happiness of the day dashed and spoiled by a few peevish words. With Maggy standing fetlock deep in kingcups, Patrick said quietly, "I am sorry for that. I'm afraid Lavinia was always inclined to be pettish if she did not have her way."

"It was natural that she should wish you to stay," returned Ann gently. "And natural, too, that she should be a little spoiled, so lovely as she is. It must always have been difficult to deny her anything."

"But much better for her ultimate happiness if someone had found the determination to do it occasionally. She has everything that a woman could wish for. Her husband adores her and panders to her lightest whim. And for all he's a south-country-man, Stephen Conroy's a very decent sort of fellow." He broke off—looked at Ann and smiled. "She even has the house—the neighbour's house that she always coveted. But it seems that she is still discontented."

There was nothing one could say to that. She could only be thankful when he turned his horse and started back up the lane, and that Philip, waited for them impatiently by the Lodge gate, was full of eager talk about his adventures with Sam. That amiable guardian, grinning all over his freckled face, accepted with dexterity the coin that Patrick slid into his grubby fist and waved them off with an injunction to Philip to 'come again soon.'

By the time that Philip had displayed the pheasant's tail feathers presented by Sam and now thrust rakishly through his cap, described the squirrel's drey that his ally had shown him, and proudly announced that he had counted seven baby oak trees, the constraint left by the encounter with Lady Conroy had been successfully banished.

A small boy has to make the most of a birthday. Grown-ups are not often so indulgent. So it was past nine o'clock before Ann finally persuaded Philip to bed. But at least he was too sleepy to demand a story. Ann herself was physically weary. It had been a long day. But her perturbed mind would not yield to the

129

demands of her tired body. She wrapped a shawl round her shoulders, and on the pretext of ensuring that the hens were safely fastened up, slipped out into the yard.

Having conscientiously checked the safety of the poultry run, she went through the gate into the kitchen garden. No one—unspecified—would think of looking for her there at that time of night. A little quirk of dry humour curled her mouth as she softly latched the gate behind her. In books, the heroine invariably betook herself to the rose arbour or to some classical marble grotto, when she felt the onset of romantic yearnings. How very appropriate, then, that workaday Ann Beverley must make do with cabbages and potatoes! Best to remember, she thought soberly, that she was not the kind of girl to attract romance. And set herself to exact and careful recollection of that strange experience on the bank of the Dee.

She could recall every word. And after a brief period of reflection she was convinced that she had not dreamed them. Convinced, too, that they had been addressed to her, even if she had not been intended to hear them. He had *not* been invoking Lady Conroy, or he would not have spoken of scarred hands.

That point settled to her satisfaction, what was she to make of it? Since coming to High Garth she had been much too busy to fall in love. She had, she admitted, been strongly attracted to Patrick Delvercourt at their first meeting. But in their busy lives there had been little opportunity for intimacy to grow. She was startled to discover, now that she came to think about it, how much he had come to dominate her life. He was her employer—yes. But it was a shock to realize that she never thought of him in that light. Working *with* a man—*for* a man, whichever it was,

130

seemed to be an excellent way of getting to know him without overmuch talk. She had thought herself in love with High Garth and an existence untrammelled by rigid convention. How if, all unaware, it was the man that she had come to love?

She pushed the thought aside, only to make way for one far more discomfiting. There had been something sadly renunciatory about Patrick's remarks. They had seemed to indicate that he found her desirable, but they carried no suggestion that he meant to make her an offer. And for herself? Would she accept? Well—there was small use in considering that at this stage. To be sure, she would ask nothing better than to spend the rest of her life at High Garth. But one didn't marry a house. Why! That would make her as bad as Lady Conroy! Poor Mr. Delvercourt. Patrick. She tried the name in a half whisper. Was he never to be loved for himself alone? And just for a moment she allowed herself to picture his face as she had seen it in that moment of wakening. Even at the memory her heart seemed to beat faster, her lips curved to an answering tenderness.

Miss Beverley, who had decided several years ago that romance was not for her, shook herself impatiently. This was no time to be falling into lovelorn megrims. If she could do no better than this, she might as well go to bed.

She paused, as always, beside a sweet-briar that clothed the end of the laithe, absently rubbing its leaves between her fingers and appreciatively sniffing the delicious new-apple scent. A little wandering breeze caught the fringe of her shawl and mischievously tangled it among the briar branches.

She sought to release the delicate strands. Patrick, coming swiftly round the corner of the laithe, ran full tilt

131

into her and flung his arms around her as much to steady her on the impact as to preserve his own balance.

For one breathless, timeless moment they rested so, Patrick drawing her close as instinctively as she clung to him and raised her face for his kiss. But the very simplicity of her surrender jerked him back to awareness. Instead of responding as inclination urged, he only rubbed his cheek gently against hers and swiftly released her.

"Janet sent me to hunt for you," he explained lightly. "She quite thought you had been gobbled up by a marauding fox, or, at the very least, shut in the poultry shed. That latch *does* jam occasionally."

Ann was thankful to stoop over the disentangling of the fringe. Even in the fading light he could scarcely fail to notice the shamed colour that burned in her cheeks. Her fingers shook and fumbled their task but he made no attempt to help her, waiting quietly till she had done and then strolling back to the house at her side. He did not, however, go in with her, for which she could only be grateful, and Janet, after one glance at her face, started scolding about people who never knew when they had done too much, and crossly adjured her to get herself to bed or she'd be fit for nothing in the morning.

Around dawn she woke, refreshed and calmed by her deep sleep. Somewhere in the mazes of that sleep, confidence had returned. Quietly, now, she reviewed the events of yesterday. And came to the conclusion that Patrick Delvercourt was as much attracted to her as she—she now admitted—was to him; but that, for some absurd masculine reason—probably because he was poor—had determined that marriage was out of the question. And since he was an honourable man, only marriage would serve. She profoundly pitied his predicament. But she had no sympathy at all with his attitude, which she unhesitatingly stigmatized as "so horribly noble". Her happiness was at stake as well as his, and she, at least, had no scruples about putting up a fight for it. She yawned and stretched luxuriously, watched the light growing towards a new day, tucked one fist under her cheek and tried to plan a strategy which might overcome Patrick's resistance, until she drifted once more into peaceful slumber.

TWELVE

Three days later, Bridie came. Word of her coming had run ahead of her. Patrick, going into Dent market, brought back long awaited letters and snippets of local news, and among these was a report that Bridie and the little brown donkey that was part of her legend had been seen in Cowgill the previous week.

At once the girls began to turn out all the stockings and caps that they had knitted during the winter months. Ann was amazed at the quantity. Even old Jim produced several pairs of beautifully knitted stockings. Most people, it seemed, knitted whenever their fingers were not otherwise employed.

Bridie arrived in the afternoon just after milking was done and settled herself beside the hearth with Janet, wholly unassuming and perfectly at ease. She was a thin little wisp of a woman who looked as though a gentle breeze would blow her away. Jewel-bright dark eyes peered out from the shelter of her black straw hat. No one ever saw Bridie without her hat. It was a wide-brimmed affair of the kind worn by sailors. Out of doors it was secured to her head by a shawl tied over it. Indoors, a silver pin fastened it to the white muslin cap that she wore under it. Jenny and Meg, who regarded the old woman with a mixture of amusement at the comical figure she cut and of awe for her supernatural powers, giggled together as they scalded out the milk pans and speculated as to whether she took the hat off when she went to bed or slept sitting bolt upright. Ann hushed them, fearful lest their mockery should reach Bridie's ears, but Bridie was too absorbed in her conversation with Janet. She was the chief news-gatherer in the district and the two had a year's marriages and births and deaths to tell and exclaim over. Nor would she have cared a pin for the girls' laughter if she had heard it. Easy enough to reduce those two to a proper respect if she so chose.

This was soon seen. After supper the men-folk discreetly vanished. It was understood that tonight the kitchen was sacrosanct to women's business. Bridie inspected the knitted goods critically and bought the lot, with an approving comment on the even quality of the yarn. But since this was achieved in the spinning, which was Janet's province, it did nothing to set the twins up in their own esteem. When it came to opening her packs she was equally firm, refusing to allow the girls to buy anything that she considered unsuitable to their age and station in life. For the first time she spoke directly to Ann, drawing her attention to some delicate lace, "Which isn't the kind o' thing I usually carry, but I bought it reasonable off a poor old body that needed the money. All she knew was the lace making and few enough to buy. So if you fancied it, ma'am"—

135

Ann bought the lace and several other small odd-ments, and watched with amusement Bridie's firm management of the ebullient twins. She herself was accorded a friendly respect which she found surprising. There had been no opportunity for Bridie to be told her history, since she had been in and out of the kitchen ever since the old woman's arrival, and there was surely nothing in her workaday appearance to impress a stranger. But Bridie, treating the twins as mischievous flibbertigibbets and Janet as an equal, accorded her from the first the deference due to gentle birth.

Practical matters completed, the party gathered around the hearth with an air of eager expectancy. The great moment of the evening had arrived. Janet herself put on the kettle and brewed the tea—in itself an exceptional proceeding at an hour when they were usu-ally thinking of bed. Handle-less cups were brought down from a high shelf, and for once the tea was drunk with more haste than appreciation. Ann felt a little uneasy. The tense faces of the girls indicated a belief in Bridie's powers that could be dangerous to their peace of mind.

But the opening procedure was decorous enough. The tea drunk, each participant must take her cup between both hands, swirl it three times about—in the direction of the sun, never withershins—and invert it over the saucer.

The telling began. The girls first, since obviously their impatience would brook no delay. To Ann's relief it seemed very much the usual stuff of fortune telling. She could see little harm coming from a prophecy of early marriage for Meg—who blushed delightedly at the prospect—or a promise of travel and change for Jenny, who seemed equally pleased. She prepared to

136

listen indulgently to her own future as Bridie saw it. Perhaps it was the soothsayer's promise of a journey and a wedding in the near future that startled her into half belief. For how could Bridie have known that Barbara's letter had brought directions for her journey, or that the wedding was fixed for the first week in September? She had not even mentioned it to Janet.

There was to be a meeting with two gentlemen, both thin, but one tall and the other short, both of whom would influence her future. That was more the sort of thing one expected. But it was the final prophecy that distressed her.

"And 'tis not for so very much longer ye'll be calling High Garth home," pronounced Bridie mournfully. "Changes be coming. Look at that!" She indicated a powdering of tiny tea particles in Ann's cup. "But 'tis good fortune. Back in your rightful place ye'll be."

Ann could scarcely protest that High Garth *was* her rightful place—the best place in the world, so long as it held the man she loved—but her feelings were plain to be seen, and were promptly endorsed by a chorus of protest from Janet and the girls.

"I can only be telling what I'm after seeing," insisted Bridie, "but if you'll let me look in your hand, ma'am, I'll be learning more."

But Ann wasn't at all sure that she wanted to hear any more on those lines even if she didn't really believe it, and said that first she wanted to hear Janet's fortune, and Janet, though she declared herself too old for such cantrips, was very willing.

Bridie smiled contentedly over this cup. "Here's good fortune indeed! 'Tis all around you. Oh—there's doubts and difficulties first, but they're soon by with, and you'll see happiness come to those you love and share it with them. And there's a journey," she added, "a short one, and it's a bit off yet."

"And that's as well," retorted Janet tartly. "The only journey I'm like to take will be to the grave yard and I'm in no hurry for that. Old I may be, but I've still plenty to do before I start goffering my shroud. But I liked that other bit you said about happiness all around me. Say it again."

After Bridie had complied, it was Janet who returned to the question of Ann's future. "Let her read your hand, love," she urged. "None of us wants to think of you leaving High Garth. Maybe your own hand'll tell a different tale."

So Ann surrendered her hands to Bridie's inspection, and that wise woman, sensing the tension in the girl, talked placidly about the art of palmistry, indicating the main lines in the hand, explaining their significance, and pointing out the difference between the left and right hands of the same subject, which they could all see. "The left shows what you were born with, the right what you've made of it," she summed up, and fell silent, studying Ann's hands intently, now that they lay relaxed and trusting in her hold.

It was some time before she spoke again, and when she did, a close observer might have noticed that though she still held Ann's hands lightly in hers, her gaze was now fixed on the glowing heart of the fire, the bright eyes hooded by the wrinkled lids. Her voice came slow and hesitant at first, its lilting accent muted to a gentle monotone that was oddly impressive.

"'Tis a strong hand, a giving hand. There's high courage in it and a deal of pride and hasty temper, and there's warmth and tenderness and loyalty beside. You've travelled far, child, and known bitter loneliness. Well do I know 'tis a home you seek, and it's a fine home you'll be after making for the man who takes you to wife. But homes are not made from sticks and stones, my dearling. 'Tis the heart of your man you must win, and he proud and stubborn as yourself. Yet in the end it shall be well with you. Gold in plenty you shall have and noble rank besides. Yes, when you have forgotten your pride and gone down into the dark waters, you shall have your heart's desire."

She fell silent. And such was the spell she had woven about them that not even the twins moved or spoke until Janet leaned forward to put another peat on the fire.

"Well that's a fine fortune to be sure," she said drily. "It certainly sounds as though we at High Garth will be bidding you farewell, for there's no gold to be gleaned in *these* parts."

Bridie did not answer. Her face was drawn in lines of great weariness. Janet put a kindly hand on her arm. "You've tired yourself out with pleasuring us. Come now. Meg will heat some milk for your cordial. Then you shall smoke a pipe in comfort before you sleep."

Meg ran to do as she was bid. Jenny said in a disappointed tone, "But I *did* want to hear more about Miss Ann's fortune. Hers was much the most exciting. Do you suppose she'll marry a prince?"

"She'll need to travel far indeed, if she's to find one worthy of a decent lass," said Janet with unusual cynicism. "I doubt she'll have to settle for a mere duke or maybe a belted earl"—Her voice trailed off into silence. She stood for an appreciable moment with her mouth half open, an oddly arrested expression on her face. "But there's still the gold," she muttered, and stooped to see if the milk was hot enough.

139

Bridie seemed much restored by the cordial, compounded from the hot milk, seasoned with nutmeg, butter and sugar, and suitably diluted by the addition of a brown syrupy liquid from a bottle in her pack. She lit her pipe and sat puffing peacefully, but she would have no more truck with fortune telling. When Jenny teased her for more details of Ann's future, and, drawing a blank here, asked mischievously what she could see in her own future, she scowled and said sombrely, "No wise woman reads her own future, girl. Think! *You* listen to my words and stare and giggle and believe only the part that pleases you. Nor do I always tell all that I see. Of what use to distress good friends with promises of sorrow that will surely come? But when I look into the future I see its fabric whole, with its pain and grief as well as its joy. 'Twould take a braver woman than me to seek such knowledge for herself. Though it is true"—she turned to Janet—"that there's times when I sense well enough what's coming, without seeking, just as the animals know when storm threatens and take shelter. Lately I've been uneasy with such knowledge. Change is coming. I'm thinking it's nothing bad, for it's finding myself curious that I am, rather than afraid to meet it, but it's something big."

Janet nodded respectfully. She understood premonitions and how they could cloud the spirits, even if one had not 'the sight', as Bridie had. Jenny was effectively silenced and she and Meg went off to bed in rather subdued mood.

Ann found herself uncomfortably impressed. That last speech was very convincing. Not a doubt that Bridie believed her own prophecies. Not a doubt, either, that she had come close to the truth where Ann was concerned. Oh—not the bits about rank and fortune, of course. Those were nonsense, prompted by Bridie's generous Irish optimism. But the part about sticks and stones not making a home, and about winning the heart of a man who might be proud and obstinate, had shown a dangerous gift of insight. It occurred to Ann that she had best tread warily while the bright dark eyes were watching. Whatever her mystic powers, Bridie, as her son-in-law was very fond of saying, could see further through a millstone than most.

THIRTEEN

Bridie was persuaded to stay over another night 'to rest her weary bones', though as far as Ann could see it was little enough resting that she did. She begged leave to help milk, explaining that she'd not milked a beast this many a year past and wanted to see if she still had the knack of it. And Will, who always declared that cows would hold back their milk from a stranger, was hugely delighted at the success of her coaxing fingers and crooning voice. Then she was at the churning, murmuring words of power to make the butter come quickly. And then, after a long conference with Janet, she vanished, accompanied by Jenny carrying a basket, to return some time later with a quantity of herbs and blossoms.

"Couldn't find any elder flowers," she complained, "so late in the season and all the fruit setting. But there was groundsel a-plenty and that will help. Can I be using the fire for a while, Miss Beverley?"

Ann watched curiously as the herbs were put in a pan with some lard and cream and Bridie proceeded to stir and pound the weird mixture over the low fire, but Philip clamouring for her assistance at that point, over the difficult business of subtracting seven from three, missed the final stages of manufacture. Consequently she stared in surprise at the two little pots that were presented to her after supper that night. They held a smooth creamy substance of a delicate greenish tint, smelling deliciously of rose water. *That* must have come out of Bridie's pack, thought Ann, for no one at High Garth possessed anything so frivolous.

"Now you'll use this every night," instructed Bridie, "and plenty of it. Janet has found some gloves that belonged to Mr. Patrick's mother, so no need to fear that it will soil the sheets."

Instinctively Ann glanced down at her hands. They *were* roughened by the unaccustomed work that they had done recently.

"Yes," nodded Bridie. "And Janet here was after telling me that you're going to a grand wedding next month. You'll want your hands smooth and white for that, won't you, now? Meg is going to do the baking for the week before you go. Time she learned to manage a brick oven, isn't it, Meg, me dearling? It's knowledge she'll be needing soon enough."

Meg blushed furiously but was understood to say that she was very willing, if Miss Ann would show her what to do. Ann thanked Bridie for her thoughtful kindness but protested that she could not sit for a whole week with idle hands, to which Janet promptly retorted that there was plenty of mending to be done, a task that would not hinder the healing work of the herb balm, not to mention Master Philip's lessons. Patrick put an end to the argument by saying quietly,

"You must certainly follow Bridie's advice, Miss Beverley, after she has gone to so much trouble. Nor must you shame us, here at High Garth, by appearing at your sister's wedding with toil-worn hands."

It was gently spoken, but it was an order. Ann subsided meekly. She had taken pains to keep out of his way as much as possible since Philip's birthday, pinning her hopes to the probability that he would miss her when she went away and would overcome whatever foolish scruples were holding him back. Meanwhile a maidenly reserve seemed to be sound policy, as well as soothing to her pride. She still blushed when she remembered the confiding way in which she had lifted her mouth for his kiss. *That* should not happen again, she vowed fiercely.

The talk ran on in leisurely fashion over the small happenings of the day. Janet was proudly informing Bridie that they had clipped over a hundred sheep that summer, "the fleeces of good quality, too." Will had put up some low obstacles in the small croft so that Jigs and Philip might learn to jump, and Jenny was teasing Meg over some mysterious message concerned with young Robert Alder. Meg's blushes and the soft glow in her eyes seemed to lend substance to Bridie's hints. Ann could not help feeling the prick of envy. Meg was not yet sixteen, but already her future seemed secure. Some would say she was over young to be thinking of marriage, but Far Riggs needed a mistress and if the young couple remained constant in their affections there was nothing to prevent an early wedding. Not for a year at least, Janet had thought, when she and Ann had discussed the frequency with which Robert turned up at High Garth. "Not before she's seventeen. She's scarcely got her growth yet, and still plenty to learn about managing a household. But if they're both of the same mind in a year's time, then I reckon we'll see a wedding. Young Robert might ha' looked higher, but Meg's a good lass and not portionless. Her dad's always been a saving sort of man."

Ann sighed, quite unconsciously, and wished that her own future was equally clear-cut and promising. Patrick's quiet voice ended her reflections.

"Has your sister set the date of her wedding yet, Miss Beverley?"

Rather diffidently Ann outlined the arrangements that Barbara had suggested. A carriage would be sent for her—the road as far as Dent was quite reasonable —and Barbara assured her that she could perfectly rely on the abigail and the coachman who would have charge of her journey. Both had been for many years in Broughton service. She must bring a night bag, since it would be necessary to lie one night in Lancaster, but nothing else, since the trunk that she had left with her sister had already been unpacked and her clothes were awaiting her arrival. It seemed unnecessary to enlighten the present company as to Barbara's views, freely expressed, on the wardrobe that she had brought with her to High Garth. Instead she said that her sister would like her to travel a week before the wedding, if she could be spared.

"There will be many small services that I can do for her—and a vast deal of talking to be done," she smiled. "Also I am to be bride's maiden, and although the dress has been made to my measurements, some slight adjustment may be needed." And then, her burden discharged, she twinkled mischievously at Janet and Bridie, since she dared not look at Patrick, and finished demurely, "You would not have me disgrace High Garth by appearing before the company in an ill-fitting gown, would you?"

Janet looked slightly shocked, but Bridie grinned. What Patrick might have said was unfortunately lost in the clamour of the twins, demanding to know exactly what the dress was to be like. By the time that Ann had eventually pacified them with a promise to bring the dress back with her so that they could see for themselves, he said only that the arrangement seemed to him a very sensible one. If she would write to her sister accepting the suggestions, he would see that the letter was sent off the next time he went to Dent.

With Bridie's departure the household settled back into its usual routine. It was a quiet time as regards seasonal work, both indoors and out. Save for periodic bursts of wedding fever from the twins punctuated by enquiries from Janet as to the efficacy of the herb balm, the days passed placidly, though the last week, during which Meg undertook the cooking and baking provided one or two hilarious surprises.

At one time Philip had shown some interest in the forth-coming wedding, his enquiries being chiefly concerned with what the wedding guests would have to eat and how many horses the Broughtons kept. But since Ann could provide only speculative suggestions on the first head and none at all on the second, his interest soon waned. The day before she left was a busy one, so many last minute instructions as she must leave for Meg, her packing to be done and her room to be left orderly. Moreover, despite her affection for High Garth, she was looking forward to the reunion with Barbara and sang as she worked, a gay, eager girl with a holiday dawning. Philip probably had some justification for feeling himself neglected. He reacted as might have been expected, passing through every stage of naughtiness from the sullen to the defiant. By supper time he had quarrelled with both the twins and been slapped by Janet. His brother's presence at the table checked any further outburst, though his hot cheeks and tightly folded lips, not to mention the absence of his usual chatter indicated that his mood was still stormy. Patrick eyed him thoughtfully but made no comment. Ann, guiltily aware that the child's behaviour was partly her fault, tried to mend matters by asking if he might ride with them as far as Dent next day. "If the day is fine," she added hastily, when Patrick looked as though he might refuse. "At least, then, you would know where he was."

"True," admitted Patrick. "But not if he means to bring *that* Friday face with him. It would frighten the horses."

Fortunately the much-injured Philip had a mouthful of hot dumpling at that moment, and by the time he had disposed of it, Patrick's assent to the proposal was somehow taken for granted. Ann was duly thankful. She had her own reasons for not wishing to ride alone with Mr. Delvercourt at the present stage of affairs.

With the object of removing Philip from the scene before his sulky demeanour could jeopardize the arrangement, she tried to coax him into going to bed early, an enterprise that might have proved disastrous had not Patrick intervened, asking Jenny if she would be so good as to see to Philip for once as there were one or two matters that he wished to settle with Miss Beverley before she left.

Ann preceded him into the parlour rather nervously, wondering what he could have to say, but it seemed that he wanted only to give her the quarter's salary that would fall due at the end of September, and then to enquire, rather shyly, if she had funds sufficient to meet any expenses that she might incur during her absence. "You may wish to make some purchases while you are within reach of shops, and there will be vails to the servants, while there is always the possibility that some minor mishap to your carriage may cause you to spend another night on the road. I would be happy to advance you next quarter's salary if you so wish."

Ann forgot all about the meekly respectful demeanour on which she had decided. Natural impulse had its way. "You shall do no such thing," she told him indignantly. "Already I am overpaid, for this quarter's money is not due until the end of the month." And then the comical side of the situation struck her and she said mischievously, "How if I did not come back? Your money would be gone. You should not be so confiding, sir."

An answering gleam lightened his sombre expression. "In that case," he told her severely, "I would have you pursued with all the rigour of the law, and apprehended. I don't know what the penalty would be for such a shocking crime. Transportation at the very least, I should imagine."

In this lighthearted mood, with the impalpable barrier that he had set between them at least temporarily forgotten, she found him quite irresistible.

"And if the officers of the law did not find me?" she tempted.

He frowned judicially. "A nice point," he conceded. His face lit with laughter. "Ah! Now I see it all. *This* is why you refused to give me Mr. Fortune's direction. The whole thing is a deep laid plot. Very well, then. I shall distrain on the goods and chattels that you leave behind!"

"The silver thimble that Mama gave me, and the locket with the likeness of Papa?" she enquired seriously, entering into the spirit of the thing.

"That I have not yet decided. But I shall certainly distrain on those intimidating caps of yours. It is positively wicked to cover your pretty hair at your age. I'll wager you won't do so at Mickleford Hall."

At that interesting moment the parlour door burst open and a small figure in a rumpled nightshirt hurled itself at Ann, sobbing so bitterly that it was some minutes before she could cuddle him into coherence.

"She said I was a horrid spoilt b-brat," he hiccoughed, "and it would s-serve me right if you didn't come back."

"So you are horrid, sometimes," said Ann cheerfully. "Everyone is. I was pretty horrid myself this morning, and I daresay even your brother has his moments"— this with a propitiating twinkle for Patrick. "But you're not spoilt. As for being a brat—my Papa was used to call me a pestiferous brat when he was feeling especially fond of me—so no need to trouble your head for that."

This categorical reassurance exerted a highly beneficial effect on the sufferer. He heaved a deep, shuddering sigh and nuzzled a rather smeary face against Ann's shoulder. "And you *will* come back, won't you?"

"Of course I will. Why! I'm leaving all my clothes behind, so I *must* come back, mustn't I? And what's more, when I do, I shall expect you to know *all* your tables, right up to the six times," she finished severely.

Her matter-of-fact manner was far more comforting than honeyed promises. His face brightened and he began eagerly, "And then there will be pig-killing and lovely brown sausages, and I shall help you to make the plum pudding for Christmas"—

"And meanwhile there is a very grubby face to be washed again and a long overdue bed awaiting a lad who must be up betimes tomorrow," put in Patrick, and scooping the child on to his shoulder carried him off upstairs.

Ann lingered in the parlour, deep in thought. In any case, she told herself, she could scarcely walk out leaving the interview unfinished. It was a pity that Philip should have come in just when things were going so well. If only Patrick's lighter mood would persist!

Alas! Though he was not gone above five minutes his manner upon his return was very different. He seemed remote, serious; his voice gentle but impersonal.

"I hope you will not refine too much upon that little demonstration," he said. "It had occurred to me that while you were staying with your sister some opportunity of more suitable employment might arise. If that should be the case, then you must not feel yourself in any way bound to High Garth. Philip is much attached to you, but a small boy's memory is short. You must not permit your affection for him to cloud your judgement. In a year or so he will be going to school, and I am sure you have realized by now that you cannot remain here indefinitely. I myself, a little while ago, voiced sentiments closely allied to Philip's. I was gravely at fault, entirely selfish. Of course we do not wish to lose you, but if it is to your advantage, then you must go, and neither affection nor misguided loyalty must be allowed to hinder."

No answer. Only the animation faded from her expression so that her face put him in mind of a flower, tight closed against some clumsy, bumbling insect. Much as he loved her he found this dumb obstinacy infuriating. Did she not understand that he wanted only her happiness and security? That it was like tearing the heart out of his breast to send her away, but that sooner or later it must be done? It seemed an age before she bowed her head and said gently, "I will remember, sir."

It sounded submissive enough, but he knew her too well. He said sternly, "You will be wise to do so." And then, on a softer note, "Meanwhile, unless you send word of any change in your plans, I shall expect you back in two weeks' time."

FOURTEEN

There was a good deal to be said for a life of luxury after all, thought Ann ruefully. It was blissful to take a bath whenever one wished without having to pump, heat and carry every drop of water, let alone the messy business of emptying it away again afterwards. Delightful, too, to sit down to a meal that one had neither planned nor prepared, and to experiment with Barbara's pretty creams and lotions as a change from Bridie's brew, effective though the latter had proved. She studied her hands critically. Dear Janet and Bridie! The twins, too. Everyone had done so much to ensure that she looked her best. Her present enjoyment of the fleshpots seemed positively traitorous.

But after a day or so she began to find the time hang heavily on her hands. Lady Broughton was a very capable woman. The arrangements for the wedding and for the guests who would be staying at the

Hall had been carefully planned to the last detail. Her staff was adequate and well trained, and it was very obvious that any offer of assistance would be presumptuous. Since Barbara was often occupied with the sewing maids who were making last minute adjustments to her new dresses, there were long periods of boring inactivity. Ann soon wearied of studying the pages of fashion journals which described gowns that she could not afford, and of strolling in perfectly kept grounds where gardeners seemed to lurk behind every bush as though defying one to pluck a single bloom. Having written to Janet to tell of her safe arrival, she had no more letters to write. Sir Henry Broughton had sought refuge from the encroachments of caterers, dressmakers, hired musicians and the like by shutting himself in his library, and she did not like to intrude upon him there. In any case this perfect, golden September weather should not be spent in stuffy rooms. It was likely to be of brief duration. Already there was hint of morning crispness, an evening chill that made a fire in one's bedroom an agreeable luxury.

Lady Broughton, thoughtful hostess, suggested that she might like to drive into the village. The shops were nothing, of course, by London standards, but there was one linen-draper who was not wholly unworthy of patronage. His prices, too, were moderate. Ethel could be spared to go with her. Oh, dear me no! Of course she could not go alone. The village was all of two miles away. And Ethel could be spared more easily than a footman.

Ann submitted to the inevitable and was duly driven into the village in the barouche, wryly amused that it required the services of the second coachman, an abigail and a pair of horses to transport her over a distance that, at High Garth, she would certainly have been expected to cover on her own two feet.

Ethel, the maid who had been appointed to wait on her during her visit, was not much older than the twins, but a good deal more sophisticated. It had not taken her long to assess Miss Barbara's sister as 'one o' the pleasant kind' with no niffy-naffy ways and not above enjoying a little friendly conversation with her attendant, and she was delighted with the prospect of an outing to the shops.

Perhaps it was because of her six months' deprivation that Ann found those shops a good deal more attractive than she had been led to expect. She wanted to buy one or two small gifts and was pleased to find the prices well within the limits of her slender purse. Janet and the twins were easy. With Ethel's enthusiastic assistance she bought two little china bowls that held solid perfume. Their scent seemed to bear little relationship to the flowers painted on the lids, but they were sweet without being sickly and when the perfume was finished they would serve for holding pins and small oddments. A fine linen handkerchief for Janet and a tiny flask of lavender water—the lavender water *was* rather expensive—left only Philip to be provided for. Here she ran into difficulty.

Had he been a little older—or her own means adequate to the purchase—she could have bought him a pair of skates, a saddle for Jigs, or even a gun. But toys for younger children were sadly lacking in variety. In the end she bought a whistle, reflecting that the gift would be highly unpopular with the other residents of High Garth, and a little glass sphere which enclosed a tiny house, a fir tree and two miniature figures. It was actually a paper weight, but Ann remembered her own childish delight in a similar bauble that had belonged

154

to her father. When you shook it, a realistic snow storm sprang up, veiling the figures in drifting flakes. Philip would love it.

Her last call was at the linen-draper's. Just one dress length, and she would make it herself during the winter evenings. Something a little brighter than her sober greys and browns.

Lady Broughton had been right. The shop was remarkably well stocked. It was plain that it catered to the local gentry. Ann looked wistfully at the rich silks and velvets which were the shopkeeper's pride, but good sense as well as straitened means put them out of court. What use were silks and velvets on a Dales farm in winter? Her employer *might* think that she looked becomingly. He was more like to think that she had run mad! Nor was such ostentation likely to recommend her as a thrifty helpmeet who would be perfectly contented with farm life!

She choose eventually a soft golden brown kerseymere. Brown *again*, she thought regretfully. But it was a very different brown. As one turned it about it glowed almost buttercup yellow. "Done in the twilling," explained the proprietor, only too happy to expound upon his mystery to an interested listener. "A certain number of the yellow strands are included in the weft." He turned the material about to show her the reverse side with its positive yellow hue. "If you wish to pick up the lighter shade with your buttons and trimmings, ma'am, match it to this."

With Ethel carrying the parcel she went back to the carriage well pleased with all her purchases. They discussed at some length the choice of a style that would make up well in the soft fabric, and then Ethel began to speak of the guests who would start arriving tomorrow. The Hall would be crammed to the eaves with those who were staying for two or three days and their personal attendants, and accomodation had been booked in every decent inn for miles around. No less a person than the Earl of Encliffe himself was to honour the occasion with his presence.

"He *is* Mr. Jack's godfather, of course, but still," proclaimed Ethel reverently. "And him to stay two nights at least!" It was plain that she found this prospect of vicarious grandeur quite stunning. It even silenced her for so much as a minute. But she soon continued her enumeration of the various lesser guests who were expected, explaining briefly how they were connected with the family and occasionally, since Miss Beverley might be counted upon to allow her a certain degree of license, throwing in a shrewd comment on their foibles. With amused interest Ann heard what a pity it was that the Countess of Encliffe would not be accompanying her lord.

"But then, she never goes nowhere. She's what they call an 'eggsentric' though what eggs has to do with it I'm sure I don't know, because its animals that she's mad after. There's never a sick or injured creature on their land but she takes it in and nurses it. And not just decent useful animals, neither, but wild ones and even vermin. They do say as she has a tame otter that follows her like a dog, but that I'd not be knowing. Milady says it's a sad pity she never had no children, which 'ud have given her something better to do, let alone there not being no heir to the title. But that's the way it is, so *she'll* not be coming to the wedding."

Ann allowed the girl's chatter to flow over her, hearing about half of it. Mention of a *real* earl had taken her back to the kitchen at High Garth, to Bridie's prophecy and Janet's scathing comments. She wondered, half smiling, if the two gentlemen who were to influence her future would be among the wedding guests.

"And Sir Stephen and Lady Conroy," said the voice beside her, startling her back to full and dismayed attention. "He was at school with Mr. Jack, and Lady Conroy is pretty as a picture and dresses very smart. 'S a good thing Miss Barbara is so dark, 'cos Lady Conroy'll shine all the blondes down and no mistake."

She then realized that this was scarcely a tactful remark to address to one who was undoubtedly a blonde, and subsided into blushful silence, but since at that moment they drew up at the door of the Hall, Ann was spared the necessity of putting her at ease. In the bustle of gathering up the packages any slight awkwardness was quickly forgotten.

It was ridiculous to feel apprehensive over Lavinia Conroy's coming. To be sure, the lady's manners scarcely evoked pleasurable anticipations, but they would probably be a good deal more conciliatory under the present circumstances. Useless to rely on not being recognized. Her height and colouring were sufficiently distinctive to make it unlikely, and the fact that she had been in Patrick's company would undoubtedly make her memorable to this particular lady. Uneasily she wondered if Lady Conroy had made enquiries about her standing at High Garth and thought it very probable that she had. Well? She had nothing to be ashamed of. The Broughtons were perfectly well aware of her situation, though it might not be very comfortable for them to have a maliciously garbled version retailed to their friends. She wished that there had been an opportunity of asking Ethel how long the Conroys were staying and whether or no they were to be house guests.

This omission she remedied when the girl came to help her dress for dinner, carefully prefacing the enquiry with one about a school friend of hers and Barbie's so that it should not have too much particularity. The answer was only partly satisfactory. The Conroys were staying only one night—they were on their way south, and it would be foolish to set out on so long a journey after the wedding—but they *were* staying in the house, which would make avoidance virtually impossible. Ann masked her concern by making a smiling remark about the extent of Ethel's knowledge of the histories and movements of the guests, which the girl accepted in all seriousness, explaining shyly that it was her ambition to be maid to Miss Barbara herself, in due course, and that to fill such a post successfully it was necessary to know as much as possible about the world in which your mistress moved.

"To know, but not to tell," she concluded solemnly, as one affirming a first principle, and lapsed into silence as she gave her whole attention to the elegant coiffeur that she was creating for the bride's sister.

FIFTEEN

On the following day, the eve of the wedding, Ann was at last gathered in to the ranks of the workers. She and Barbara spent the forenoon arranging the flowers in the reception and guest rooms, and so impressed was Lady Broughton by their artistic achievements that she invited Ann to go down to the church after luncheon to put any necessary finishing touches to the flowers there. Barbara, of course, could not be spared. The first guests would be arriving soon and she must be on hand to take her share in receiving them.

Rather reprehensibly Ann dismissed the carriage, telling herself that it might be required for some other purpose, and spent a contented afternoon in the church, the air filled with the scent of great masses of yellow and white chrysanthemums and white and gold lilies, and strolled back to find the Hall already seething with excitement. Upward of thirty guests would sit down to dinner, in addition to the family. Feeling grubby and untidy she managed to slip up to her room unperceived and so did not meet any of them until she went down to dinner.

Since it was a very formal affair, Ann supposed that the gentleman in the place of honour beside his hostess must be the Earl of Encliffe. And there was Papa Fortune on her other hand. All the rest were strangers.

It seemed only proper that Papa Fortune should seek her out when the gentlemen eventually joined the ladies in the drawing room, though it was rather surprising that he should bring the Earl with him. As they came down the long room together she was suddenly seized by the most ridiculous notion. So ridiculous that she was hard put to it to restrain a chuckle, and it was a merry, smiling face that she lifted to greet them. For here, undoubtedly, were the two gentlemen of Bridie's prophecy. And though it was certainly possible that Papa Fortune might yet influence her future, it seemed highly unlikely that his tall companion would do so.

The unaffected enjoyment in her face struck pleasantly on both gentlemen, though it was possibly fortunate that they did not guess its cause. There was a note that might almost have been pride in Mr. Fortune's voice as he presented the Earl.

"My second step-daughter. The rebel and runaway," he added severely, but there was no real reproof in his tone. Ann glanced at him curiously. In the three years since she had last seen him, he seemed to have mellowed a good deal.

"So you informed me," agreed the Earl gently. "But do you think it quite kind to bait her with such accusations when she is in no case to defend herself?

Come, Miss Beverley, pay no heed to him. You shall take me to the small salon if you will be so kind, and show me these miniatures which my hostess has been describing to me."

Ann hesitated for a moment, but surely there could be nothing improper in accepting such an invitation from one who was old enough to be her father. She put her fingers on the proffered arm and allowed him to escort her from the room.

He had not missed the tiny hesitation, and laughed softly. "You are very right, Miss Beverley. In my heyday it would have been much wiser to decline that invitation. But nowadays I am a reformed character, I promise you. My motives, if not wholly disinterested, are perfectly chivalrous."

Ann eyed him thoughtfully. One scarcely expected that bantering tone from a gentleman of exalted rank on such short acquaintance. She was not discomfited, but she was wary.

"Not wholly disinterested?" she repeated, brows lifting.

He laughed. "No, indeed. I look to you to save me from a very boring evening. And no need to draw that reproving mouth. My fellow guests are very worthy—wholly delightful. But I have been doing the polite since early afternoon, and enough is enough. You and I will agree at the outset that the bride is perfectly charming, the bridegroom a very fine fellow and the marriage obviously destined to succeed. Then we may forget them and turn to our own amusement. Your step-papa tells me that your present situation is with a farming family who live in some very remote dale. Surely you must have had experiences—adventures, even—quite out of the common way. Behold me, all attention!"

She found him a delightful companion. He had the knack of drawing her out without seeming to pry, and at the end of half an hour they were on very easy terms. She was a little surprised to find so important a personage even mildly interested in the small affairs of life on a Dales farm, and was inclined to ascribe his attitude to inherent good manners rather than to genuine concern, but she had no fault to find with that. Why *should* he be sincerely concerned? He made her feel that she was holding his attention, that her remarks were witty and entertaining, her opinions of value. Under this skilled handling she relaxed and glowed into something approaching beauty. The cool grey eyes, appraising her more closely than she guessed, were well pleased with what they saw. By the time that Mr. Fortune came seeking them, the Earl was gravely describing some of his wife's animal protegees and their strange ways, stories which Ann assured him would be of deep interest to her small charge. If Mr. Fortune checked briefly and swallowed his amazement at seeing this ill-assorted pair so easy together, he was swift to recover his usual poise. He had come, he explained, to tell them that in view of the next day's activities most of the ladies were retiring early, but that several of the gentlemen were proposing to while away an hour with a rubber of whist. He had thought that the Earl might like to join them.

Strolling back towards the drawing room he informed Ann, "And thanks to his lordship here, I've not had the chance of a word with you. There's one or two things I have it in mind to say, so maybe tomorrow when all the fuss is over you'll spare me half an hour of your time."

Ann agreed to it and bade them both goodnight. She went slowly up to Barbara's room, wondering once

162

again at the change in her step-father's manner. Why! He had been positively polite!

She tapped on Barbara's door and went in, wondering if her sister's customary placidity might have yielded to an understandable nervousness. Barbara was sitting on the bed, an open velvet jewel case in her hands, a slightly dazed expression on her face. She looked up as Ann came in, the shine of tears in her eyes, and held out the case wordlessly for her sister's inspection.

"Mama's pearls!" exclaimed Ann wonderingly. "His wedding gift to her."

Barbara shook her head. "No. He is saving those for you. He said it was only right, as you were the elder. But he has had them matched for me, and the pendant and brooch too. I could scarcely believe my own eyes. He just pushed them into my hands as I was bidding him goodnight and would scarcely let me thank him. And as if that were not enough, Lady Broughton let slip this afternoon that he had settled a very handsome sum of money on me. She was surprised, she said, even a little shocked, that my greeting should be so cool. Did I not realize how fortunate I was to have a stepfather of so generous a disposition? Papa Fortune! Who grudged us every penny that was not spent on necessities. He told the Broughtons that he fully approved the match and had promised Mama that I should not go dowerless to my wedding. I feel so ashamed I could weep."

So the change in Papa Fortune was not just in her imagination. Ann could only share her sister's feelings. "I suppose that's what he wants to tell me about," she said ruefully. "Mama's pearls. But why, why couldn't he have shown a tiny fraction of this generosity when we were younger? When it meant so much to have new dancing slippers or a pair or real silk stockings?"

It must have taken months, perhaps years, to match those pearls, she thought, making her own preparations for bed. There was no saying how long the plan had been in his mind, no understanding it at all. But she was too sleepy to lie long awake puzzling over her stepfather's inconsistencies.

She enjoyed Barbara's wedding. Lady Broughton's careful arrangements worked perfectly. Nobody was hot or hurried. Barbara looked lovely and very happy. The rich creamy brocade she had chosen for her wedding gown set off her dark colouring to admiration, and Ann knew that her own gown, of a delicate lilac pink, was vastly becoming. It did a good deal for one's social confidence, she discovered, to know that one looked one's best.

There was the usual delay, the usual laughter and teasing before the bridal pair left and such guests as lived in the vicinity gradually drifted away. She went slowly upstairs to tidy herself for dinner. There was no great haste, for she did not mean to change her gown. The lilac silk was far more elegant than anything else she possessed, and she would have few enough opportunities of wearing it. A mood of gentle melancholy possessed her. She was happy for Barbara, but it was sad to say goodbye to the close alliance that had linked them from birth.

Reaching the head of the stairs she lingered for a moment to make way for a hurrying abigail coming from the servants' wing with a can of hot water. The girl was a stranger and she looked flushed and harrassed. She tapped on the door of one of the principal guest rooms and vanished within, but in her haste she did not close the door properly. Ann heard a sharp-pitched feminine voice say crossly, "—just because you

164

must needs display your much-vaunted skill with the ribbons!"

"My dear, the accident would have happened just the same whoever was driving." The masculine voice was a little weary, as though its owner's patience was under considerable strain.

Ann hurried past. She had never heard Lady Conroy in a temper, but she had no doubt at all as to the owner of the peevish voice. In her absorption in the day's events, she had forgotten all about the Conroys, but she now recalled that they had not been present either in church or at the reception afterwards. No doubt when Ethel arrived she would hear all about the accident that had delayed them.

But for once Ethel failed her. She was full of the party that was to be given for the servants and of what she meant to wear, and as Ann did not like to question her directly she had to wait until the ladies retired to the drawing room after dinner to satisfy her curiosity.

If the accident had caused Lady Conroy to miss the wedding, she certainly turned it to good account now in focussing all attention upon herself. To do her justice she told it well, with considerable dramatic ability and much play of fine eyes. Quite a pity that the display was being wasted on a wholly feminine audience, thought Ann unkindly. She knew that she was prejudiced against the storyteller, but even by her own account the lady came out of the incident with little credit, though of this she seemed quite unconscious.

The Conroy chariot had been in collision with a gig driven by a young girl whose strength had proved unequal to the task of controlling a bolting horse. A window in the chariot had been shattered and its gleaming panels scratched and dented, but the damage sounded fairly superficial. The gig had lost a wheel and cracked a shaft, and both horse and driver had been cut by flying glass. Lady Conroy's abigail had tended the hysterical girl while her husband and coachman had freed the frantic horse from the wreckage of the gig.

"And we might still have been here in time for the wedding," continued the narrator plaintively, "if Sir Stephen had not insisted on driving the girl to her home, which was quite unnecessary. It's not as though she was a lady—just some farmer's daughter on her way to market—and could do nothing but weep over smashed eggs and spilt cream, and vow the horse had never done so before but she thought a hornet must have stung him. *Such* a fuss. And no one with any thought for the dreadful shock to *my* nerves."

At that point the arrival of the gentlemen caused the group around her to break up and re-form into several small knots of congenial friends. Ann drifted across to a small table standing beside the curtain-draped archway that gave on to the library. It held a collection of Chinese ivories and she examined these with interest and some amusement. Apart from Lady Conroy's vivacious chatter there was a feeling of languor in the air. Everyone was pleasantly tired. Lady Broughton, receiving the appreciative remarks of her friends with smiling serenity, presently roused herself to ask the belated guest if she would give them the pleasure of a song. Lady Conroy demurred, saying with a delightful smile that her singing was no great thing, and the invitation was not pressed.

The smile faded. An incipient frown darkened the beautiful brow, and since her husband was engaged in conversation with his host there was no one to coax or coerce the lady into a proper mode of behaviour. Seeking about her for some opportunity of venting her ill-humour, her eye chanced to light upon Ann. She rose, and rustled across the room with an air of pretty condescension.

"*Such* a surprise to meet you here, Miss Beverley," she began. "You are, I must suppose, a distant connection of the new Mrs. Broughton. I had thought you—if I had *given* the matter any thought—wholly occupied with your many duties at High Garth. Such a rara avis as you are acclaimed. Do I take you out of your depth? But no! So accomplished a young person is, I am sure, well instructed in the Latin tongue. A paragon indeed. Your neighbours have not ceased to sing your praises. Not only highly educated, but equipped with all the domestic talents and wholly devoted to the Delvercourt interest. *That* at least I believe," she put in, the charming voice suddenly raw and ugly with spite, "having seen something of it myself. And to be sure, no one ventured to say that you were a paragon of *propriety* Did you think that dung heap of a farm so remote that you might pursue your pastoral idyll unobserved? Or is it matrimony you have in mind? If that's your ambition, you're wasting your time. Patrick Delvercourt can't afford marriage, and if he could he'd scarcely pick a wench out of his own kitchen."

At first completely taken aback by the spate of venomous words, Ann's instinct to retaliate in kind was further inhibited by her position as, in some sort, her antagonist's hostess. The jibes at herself she might have ignored since they were so patently the imaginings of a petty and jealous mind. But the sneer at her beloved High Garth and the belittling references to Patrick were too much for any female spirit to endure. Her own quick temper took charge. She said hotly, "If Mr. Delvercourt chooses to marry I am sure his wife will be perfectly happy at High Garth. Unless, of

167

course, he has the misfortune to select a luxury-loving little fortune hunter who values wealth and rank above integrity and human warmth."

"Hoity-toity! Here's a high flight," smirked Lady Conroy. "These northern wastes seem to abound in non-pareils. Master Patrick is become a knight in shining armour to his kitchen wench! I suppose *he* paid for that gown you're wearing. It's easy enough, my girl, to be noble and generous at someone else's expense! You may tell your fine master, you nasty little slut, that Sir Stephen has decided not to renew his lease of the Court after next quarter day. *Then* see how much of his nobility and generosity is left."

The words struck dismay to Ann's heart. She knew how delicately the finances of High Garth were balanced, and that it was from the letting of the Court that Patrick hoped to save money for Philip's education. Wild thoughts of humble apology, even of pleading, flashed through her mind, though instinct warned that they would be worse than useless. But help was at hand, if from a rather unexpected quarter.

Standing with her back to the archway she had not noticed when the curtain was drawn aside; and her tormentor, happily absorbed in the pain that she could inflict on one who had aroused her bitterest jealousy, was equally blind. It was the tall figure of the Earl of Encliffe who stood in the opening; his cool voice that fell upon startled ears.

"Dear me!" he said blandly. "How very odd!" He raised his glass, and with its aid surveyed Lady Conroy with the impartial curiosity that one would accord to an unusual specimen, a proceeding that caused the lady to lower her gaze and to fidget with her fan. "You will forgive me, Miss Beverley?" he went on, the cool voice now rueful, apologetic. "I came to bring you a message from your step-papa, and I could not help overhearing what passed between you and this—er—young woman. In my day, you must understand, matters of business were left to *my* sex. A lady would have thought it shocking bad ton to be found discussing such a sordid affair as the renewal of a lease. But the ways of modern society are a continual surprise to me. I grow old, I fear."

Since the Earl moved in the most select circles, his approval earnestly sought by aspirants to fashion, this could only be construed as a crushing set-down, while his show of friendship towards the despised Miss Beverley merely rubbed salt into the wound. Lady Conroy flushed a dull and unbecoming red, murmured something slightly disjointed about her husband trying to catch her eye this while past, and retreated.

The Earl looked down at Ann. His expression was unexpectedly sympathetic. "Objectionable creature," he said dispassionately. "Don't let her distress you, child. In matters such as this it is her husband who will have the last word, and I can safely promise you that your employer will get fair dealing from *him* But I forget my errand. Mr. Fortune would be grateful for a quiet word with you in the library. He and I are off tomorrow, sooner than we had intended, and mean to leave betimes. We have business together in Manchester."

Ann was betrayed into showing her surprise. "Business? In Manchester?" she repeated, and then blushed and would have apologized.

The Earl smiled. "Yes. You *did* here me correctly," he assured her, completing her confusion. "Do you think me a renegade? *You* I know to be a country lover—indeed, I share your preference. But I have come to see that England's future prosperity lies, not in her lush green meadows, but in industry and commerce. We must develop and increase the products of our inventive genius, and seek wider markets. The meeting that your step-papa and I are to attend tomorrow is concerned with the development of railways—the highways of the future—which will carry the products of our mills and manufactories and foundries to the ports. But I become a dead bore. Such a lecture! Permit me, my dear young lady, to bid you farewell and good fortune. Why knows? Some day we may meet again—a hope that I shall cherish sincerely."

She curtsied and gave him her hand in farewell, thinking that she, too, would be happy to meet him again, so kindly as he had spoken to her, and went off to the library reflecting amusedly that she had not thought to hob-nob with the aristocracy when she set out from High Garth, and smiling at the thought of what he would say if he met her in working dress and the pattens that she wore in the dairy.

The smile was soon banished when Papa Fortune informed her affably that he had taken order for her return journey, and, with his customary high-handedness, had already won Lady Broughton's consent to his scheme.

"So as I was determined to see for myself this place that you're so set on," he explained, "we decided that I should take you up in my carriage when I come back from Manchester. We shall lie one night in Lancaster, and his lordship assures me that there's a very decent little inn in this place—Ghent—no —Dent, that's it. Your kind hosts will be spared the trouble of sending their carriage and servants to see you safe home. There now, what do you think of that?"

Fortunately she could find no words to tell him.

Between indignation at having her own arrangements calmly over-set and horror when she strove to visualize Mr. Fortune's impact on High Garth, she was speechless. And the plan was so sweetly reasonable, so precisely the behaviour of a careful parent, that there could be no evading it without making an unbecoming fuss. Disturbed and apprehensive, she went early to bed, thankful only that, as the Conroys, too, were leaving very early, she could avoid a further meeting with them by the simple process of remaining in her room till they were gone.

SIXTEEN

In the event, Papa Fortune proved to be an unexpectedly pleasant travelling companion, peaceable and competent. The mellowing of his disposition was inexplicable but apparently lasting, and Ann sunned herself in his unaccustomed good humour. A conversible evening in Lancaster did much to explain matters. The cheerful fire in the private parlour at the Castle Inn, an excellent meal and a tolerably smooth burgundy induced in Mr. Fortune a benign and confidential mood. He was, he informed Ann, to marry again.

"I always thought to marry Amelia," he told her. "She's my cousin, and we were brought up together after I lost my own parents when I was no more than a nipperkin. My uncle and aunt did their duty by me, there's no gainsaying, and maybe a bit over. A yeoman farmer, he was, and in a pretty prosperous way. They gave me a home and good schooling to start me off in the world. But when it came to me wanting to marry Amelia, that was different. What with us being cousins, which Uncle Nat didn't hold with such close kin marrying, and with me having no money to speak of, which Aunt Isa didn't approve, she being one with an eye to the moneybags, there were sour looks and some hard words spoken. Amelia was packed off to her Grandma's in Wales, while I went back to London with my tail between my legs. Not that I gave up. I worked like three men, and I skimped and scraped and saved every halfpenny. I thought by the time Melia was of age I'd be able to show them that I was on the way to being a man of substance, and that maybe they'd change their minds. But I reckoned without Aunt Isa. Before the year was out she had her lass saxely tied up in marriage to a wealthy widower of *her* choosing. By what I can make out he was a kind enough husband, even if he was nigh on thirty years older than her, and he left her well provided for when he died. She's no need to marry again unless she chooses. But she's neither chick nor child to care for, while *I've* only the one step-daughter left on my hands—and an independent piece *she* is!"

He directed a fierce glare at Ann, but there was a distinct twinkle in the frosty blue eyes. She was encouraged to meet the accusation with an air of innocent surprise that made him smile.

"It's a lonely business growing old alone," he went on presently. "Melia and me decided we'll see it out together. Aunt Isa's been dead this many a year, but Uncle Nat's still hale and hearty and gives us his blessing. Now that there's no danger of us breeding the idiot-children he threatened us with," he threw in, a trace of that old bitterness still audible in the cadence of his voice.

Then suddenly he grinned, hugely, as Ann had never seen him do, and added, "And has the impudence to announce that he'll condescend to make his home with us, since, he reckons, I owe him some return for his fostering care in my childhood!"

He seemed to regard this as a great joke and chuckled over it for quite some time, but presently his mood grew reflective again.

"Your mother—well—I suppose I loved her beyond the bounds of reason. She was the kind of faery creature a man dreams of. But we weren't suited. She was too fine-grained, too sensitive for a man of my stamp. I might lap her in luxury, but at every turn my dealings jarred on her. I'd see her shrink when I spoke roughly to some menial or denied some treat to you or to Barbara. But I'd been bred in a harsher mould and I couldn't change. I tried hard enough. Vowed I'd not make the same mistakes again—and made others—worse ones. There had been no treats in my childhood. The servants I had known had been just that—servants. How could I understand the devotion that links some faithful old retainer and the cherished child of the family? Or realize that a mother would rather forego some offered luxury than deny a treat to her daughters? You thought me hard, I know, but I did my best for you in my own fashion—and you, at any rate, have good reason to be grateful. Even if, some day, you marry a man of wealth and position, your servants will respect you the more for your competence."

Ann wondered what he would say if she told him that her sole ambition was to marry a penniless Dales farmer. The revelation would certainly put an abrupt and stormy end to this pleasantly domestic interlude! She said instead that he was perfectly right, and that she now valued his care for her far more justly than she had done in her heedless youth.

Much pleased by this very proper attitude, Mr. Fortune enlarged for a little while longer on his matrimonial plans and his daring notion of taking his bride to Italy for the honeymoon. When Ann finally rose to bid him goodnight, they were on better terms than they had ever known.

Preparing for bed in her comfortable room, she thought repentantly of the many times that she had rejected his counsel; of the occasions when she and Barbara had deliberately provoked him into showing himself at his worst in front of Mama. What horrid creatures children could be, she brooded. And then decided that she was becoming maudlin. Even now she would not willingly submit herself to his sole authority. She might understand him better, now that she knew the circumstances that had gone to his making, but the fact remained that they would never really see eye to eye. So she could only be thankful that his future held a promise of companionable comfort.

They set out early next day, a crisp day of early autumn, of brilliant sunshine and blue skies, that yet gave warning of coming winter in the vividly coloured hedgerows and the trees that were dappled with bronze and yellow. Mr. Fortune shivered a little and wound a scarf about his throat, but Ann's spirits seemed to mount every mile that brought her nearer to home and Patrick. Tomorrow she should see him. Had he missed her? Would she read in his face open acknowledgement of the love she believed he bore her? For the moment she forgot the difficulties that might arise from Mr. Fortune's presence, and thought only of the happiness that could await her at the journey's end, and her face glowed with such joyous anticipation that her companion studied her rapt countenance curiously. Presently he ventured a question.

"You are happy to be going back to your work? No regrets for the lazy luxurious life you are leaving?"

She laughed. "I shall miss some of my comforts very much," she confided, "but yes, I am happy to be going home."

He made no comment on the unconscious betrayal implicit in the last word, though a faint smile hovered about his mouth and he nodded as one well satisfied. Instead he made one or two desultory remarks about the passing scene, commenting approvingly on farm land that looked to be in good heart, though an eye accustomed to south country farming missed the golden stubble fields. "Mostly cattle and sheep, I suppose," he grunted. "Pity. There's no sight so fair as a field of standing corn just ripe for the sickle."

They reached Sedbergh by mid-afternoon and changed horses for the last time. Ann sniffed the clear hill air contentedly, but Mr. Fortune viewed the high fells that barred their way with deep disapproval.

"That's no kind of country for farming!" he said disgustedly. "Don't tell me this Delvercourt fellow expects to make a success of that sort of caper. He must be all about in his head." The barbaric splendour of the scenery left him unimpressed. He spoke sourly of the difficulty and expense of road building over such a terrain, and marvelled that anyone should choose to live in a wilderness when he might enjoy all the amenities of civilization in the cities.

Ann knew better than to argue. She could only be thankful that he pronounced Dent to be a snug little town, the inn that the Earl had recommended surprisingly comfortable. They were served with a good, plain dinner, which earned his approval, but the confidential atmosphere of the previous evening was lamentably missing. The genial bridegroom-elect had vanished and in his place sat the keen-eyed man of affairs. Ann was subjected to a searching inquisition as to ways and means at High Garth, an inquisition so embarrassing as the poverty of the place emerged more and more clearly, that she pleaded fatigue at the first possible moment and retired early to bed.

It was some time, however, before she slept. Tomorrow was going to be more than a little awkward. Papa Fortune had sharp eyes. Not for worlds would she have Patrick betray himself to that penetrating gaze. And there had been no opportunity to advise the folk at High Garth of her change of plan. Patrick would be expecting only herself. What would be his attitude to the intrusion of an uninvited stranger?

That problem at least was not destined to embarrass her. At breakfast a message was brought to her from Mr. Delvercourt. He regretted that he would not be able to come for her until early afternoon, and hoped that she would be able to amuse herself meantime in exploration of the little town. She looked doubtfully at her step-father and tentatively suggested a visit to the church, which was, she assured him, of considerable antiquity and very interesting. But Papa Fortune had very different ideas. He entered into negotiation with the landlord for the hire of a gig, not wishing to risk his own elegant vehicle on such dubious roads, and took her off to visit the marble mills, where he became so enamoured of a black chimney-piece that he enquired into the possibility of having one delivered to his London home. Just the thing to give the drawing room a new touch, he assured Ann enthusiastically, and he was sure that Amelia would like it of all things. By the time that he had chosen a design from the pattern book, entered into a long debate on the respective merits of sending it by carrier all the way or by sea, and embarked upon an exhaustive tour of the premises, the morning had gone. They returned to the Sun to find Patrick awaiting their arrival and already advised of Mr. Fortune's presence.

It was impossible to discover whether her return gave him any particular delight, though he greeted her warmly enough and there was mention of the eager welcome that awaited her at the farm. At least he had not betrayed himself to Papa Fortune, she consoled herself, and watched with considerable interest the meeting between the two gentlemen.

They exchanged greetings with a courtesy which did not wholly mask the deep reserve of the one, the speculative enquiry of the other. Mr. Delvercourt had already lunched, but he insisted that they should not hurry over their belated repast and sat at table with them, accepting a glass of claret, sipping in leisurely fashion and conversing on such topics as might be supposed to interest Mr. Fortune. Presently, however, he drew Ann into the conversation.

She would be sorry, he knew, to hear that Bridie had met with an accident, having fallen and broken her leg as she pursued her solitary way along the green tracks. Luckily she had been found almost at once by a party of drovers and had been carried by these rough but kindly men to a nearby inn. The broken limb was mending well, but Bridie was fretting about her inactivity, her mounting debt to the innkeeper and most of all about her donkey. Word of her distress had been brought to Will at High Garth and Patrick had sent him off at once to see what arrangements could be made for her comfort. Will's absence naturally meant more work for those left at home, hence his belated arrival.

"In fact," he concluded, "though I am loath to hurry you, Miss Beverley, we should set out soon. As it is, the girls will have to manage the milking."

There was an awkward little pause. Ann glanced uncomfortably at her stepfather. That gentleman said composedly, "How very unfortunate. I had hoped to improve my acquaintance with you, perhaps even to call upon you and see something of the home that this child prefers to mine. You will understand, I am sure, that my responsibility for the welfare of so wilful a girl is no light one. I would have liked to assure myself that she was suitably established. However, if it is inconvenient, I must abandon the scheme for the moment."

He waited hopefully. A furiously indignant Ann swallowed some hasty words on the subject of encroaching ways, not to mention the odiously patronizing indulgence of the reference to herself. Patrick's mouth twitched slightly, his eyes were amused. "But it is not in the least inconvenient, sir. You must know that *my* housekeeper is not one to be put out by the arrival of—er—unexpected guests. You will find everything in apple pie order, I promise you. I shall be honoured if you will accept the hospitality of High Garth for as long as you care to stay."

"Now that's very handsome of you," approved Mr. Fortune cheerfully. "What's more—and maybe this'll surprise you—I may even be able to lend a hand while this man of yours is away. Bred up on a farm I was, though it's more years ago than I care to think of. And that was in Wiltshire, which is what I call *real* farming country. This Will, now. He'll be your head cowman I take it?"

Patrick laughed outright. "*Sole* cowman and general handyman as well," he explained. "Before you commit yourself too far, sir, you had best know what lies before you. We will do our best to make you comfortable, but it's no fine estate that you are to visit; nor am I a wealthy eccentric playing at husbandry. High Garth is a small hill farm, and I have just two men to help me." He studied his work hardened palms. "And I may say that it's a full time job, wresting a living from my thankless acres."

There was a gleam of approval in Mr. Fortune's eyes. "Well, hard work never hurt a man yet," he pronounced dispassionately. "Though that's not to say you might not work to better purpose in a more fertile soil," and he glanced disapprovingly at the mist-wreathed fells that ringed the little town. "But that we'll see in good time."

Having won his way, he was in the best of humours, and bustled about cheerfully over his preparations, making light of every difficulty. Ann, still seething at the blatant manner in which he had angled for his invitation, wondered grimly what he would make of the democratic ways of Janet's kitchen. It was probably a good thing that the forthright Will would not be present.

In point of fact his visit caused less stir than she had feared. The twins, overawed by what they had already heard of the gentleman's consequence, were unusually subdued. Janet was her dignified self, determined that the newcomer should have no cause to complain of High Garth's hospitality, and Jim was quiet, as ever, in the presence of strangers. Even Philip, with the promise that there would be a present for him after supper, was on his best behaviour.

So, too, was Papa Fortune. He did not say a great

180

deal but it was easy to see that he was quite at home in a farmhouse. His voice actually took on something of the rustic burr that it had held in his youth, and he was promising himself a busy day of exploration on the morrow, dusk having put a stop to such an enterprise tonight.

Supper done, he accepted Patrick's invitation to sit with him in the parlour. The invitation was also extended to Ann, but she declined it on the plea of unpacking to be done, a plea heartily endorsed by young Master Philip. Never had the supper table been cleared nor the dishes washed with more helpful celerity. And never, perhaps, had such small gifts given so much pleasure. The twins danced joyously round the kitchen, comparing their gifts and hugging the giver. Janet's handkerchief must be smoothed out and refolded half a dozen times, the precious lavender water appreciatively sniffed, while Philip was so enchanted with his 'snowball', as he insisted on calling it, that after one or two experimental blasts he was persuaded to put the whistle aside for outdoor entertainment.

When the excitement had abated and a sleepy Philip had been tucked into bed, Meg and Jenny begged to see the bridesmaid's dress. A glimpse of this splendour had been vouchsafed them when they had helped unpack, but now they wanted Ann to put it on so that they could see just how she had looked.

She hesitated, not sure that she wished to run the risk of having Patrick see her tricked out in fashionable finery, however becoming. Meg said coaxingly, "While your hands are still nice," and ruefully displayed a blister on her own wrist. Ann remembered, in a warm surge of affection, all that they had done to help her look her best, and their total lack of jealousy, and against her better judgement she yielded.

"We shall have to be quick, though," she stipulated. "See—it is past nine o'clock already, and tomorrow will be extra busy. Time we were all abed."

Both girls were only too eager to help her dress, touching the silken petticoat and the rich fabric of the dress itself with shy unaccustomed fingers, Jenny proving herself surprisingly adept with buttons and hooks. As usual her hair presented a problem. Ethel had dressed it for the wedding, piling it high at the back of her head with a tiny diadem of rock crystals clasped round the knot, but there was no time for ornate hair styles tonight.

"Leave it loose," suggested Jenny, her own eyes shining more brightly than the crystals. "With that little crown on top you look just like the princess in Master Philip's story book."

Ann laughed. "More like a maypole with the garland a-top," she retorted. "Very well, then. It will save time. But do *you* run downstairs and make sure the gentlemen are still in the parlour."

Even when the scout had reported that all was safe, the three crept downstairs like conspirators, muffled giggles from the twins, Ann with fast-beating heart and hands that shook on the stair-rail. But they reached the kitchen in safety and now she could breathe freely. Patrick would certainly escort the guest to the bed-chamber that had been hastily made ready for him before he himself returned to the kitchen, as was his custom, to take order for the next day's work. That would give her ample time to make her escape.

She had forgotten the claims of hospitality. As, indeed, had Patrick himself, so long accustomed to solitary evenings. But an hour spent in the society of Mr. Fortune had reminded him that it was customary for gentlemen to sit over their wine if no better entertainment offered. He was inclined to like his guest, finding him honest and unpretentious despite his obvious confidence in his own worth. But there could be no denying that close converse with him left one feeling slightly battered and breathless. He asked personal questions with an impersonality that made it impossible to resent or evade them, and question, comment and suggestion followed one another with relentless persistence. It was as much the need for a brief escape from this catechism as the recollection of his duties as host that sent Patrick to the kitchen in search of glasses, thankful that he could still draw upon the remnant's of his uncle's cellar.

He walked in upon a scene that was unusual, to say the least of it, in that setting. Ann was standing with one foot outstretched and skirts coquettishly extended so that Janet might see the pretty satin slippers, while Jenny, perched on a stool, comb in hand, was straightening the diadem which did not sit very securely on the loosened hair. Meg was adjusting the lamp to give a better light. There was a concerted gasp of dismay and for one breath-stopping moment the actors in this tableau seemed to be frozen, their eyes fixed on the master's face. Then, with one accord, and regardless of proper deference, the twins stepped forward as though to come between Ann and the anger in those tawny eyes, for they held a fury to intimidate the boldest. Ann's own hands dropped limply to her sides, though pride insisted that she hold herself erect and outface him.

But Patrick did not at once release his wrath, though perhaps his icy courtesy hurt more than a rougher tongue.

"I beg your pardon for my intrusion," he said. "Janet, do you think you could lay your hand on two of the good glasses?" And as the old woman got up to do his bidding he turned back to Ann. "You must allow me to tell you that you look quite delightfully, Miss Beverley. It is most kind in you to give us humbler folk a glimpse of a world that is quite beyond *our* touch."

Fortunately at that point Janet came back with the glasses, for resentment of the unjust jibe had for the moment swamped Ann's misery. There was no opportunity for retort. As the door closed behind him, Meg said in a bewildered voice, "But we weren't doing anything wrong. Why was he so cross?"

Despite her own hurt and anger, Ann's instinct was to spring to the defence of the beloved. "It *is* very late," she offered. "And I suppose he thought we were wasting our time, frivolling."

"Perhaps Mr. Fortune said something to annoy him," suggested Jenny. But Janet shook her head.

"I doubt it was the sight of you in that dress," she said sorrowfully. "It would put him in mind of the kind of life he should have been leading, but for his father's folly. But don't you let it upset you, Miss Ann. He'd be sorry enough as soon as he'd said it. Because it's not your fault, and well he knows it." Nevertheless it was a rather subdued little group that made its way to bed. Perhaps Janet was the nearest in her interpretation of her master's feelings, but even she was only partly right. It was not the world of fashion that Patrick craved. Indeed he infinitely preferred his present way of life, having proved it far more satisfying than days spent in moving between town house and club, between his tailor and Tattersall's, between breakfast parties, Park parades, morning visits and the endless succession of evening entertainments. But to see the girl he loved dressed as his wife might have dressed, had it not been for his father's aberrations; to see her, warm, glowing, laughing, with her lovely hair loose about her shoulders, and to know that he could never hope to claim her as his own, had touched him on the raw. He had lashed out in helpless fury. How he endured the rest of the evening with Mr. Fortune he scarcely knew. Fortunately the older man admitted to some travel weariness and retired to bed at a reasonably early hour, assuring his host that he meant to rise early in anticipation of a full and absorbing day.

SEVENTEEN

Ann eventually cried herself to sleep. Her dreams were shattered. He did not love her. He seemed almost to hate her. Only hatred could explain those cruel words, and her one thought was escape. She must leave High Garth at the first opportunity, for to stay on in the face of such bitter aversion was more than she could endure. She slept badly and woke heavy-eyed and unrefreshed.

But work must go on, and at least everyone was too busy to comment on her sickly looks and her lack of conversation. Patrick, too, was silent, the twins unwontedly subdued, though she could not decide whether this was due to last night's unpleasantness or to shyness in the presence of a stranger. Fortunately that gentleman was in the best of spirits, even unbending so far as to compliment Jim on his weather lore, and his flow of talk covered the silence of the others.

Ann set about her tasks mechanically. There was plenty to do, since pride would not permit a sore heart to excuse indifferent cooking, but for once there was no joy in the work. And Philip, as though sensing her preoccupation, was in his naughtiest mood, employing his energies in drawing ingenious red herrings across the paths of instruction. He celebrated his release from lessons by blowing a series of ear-piercing blasts on his new whistle, startling Janet into dropping a jug of batter. Ann impounded the whistle, reminding the sinner of his promises, and he stumped off in a fit of the sullens.

Somehow the day dragged its weary length away, and at least the supper over which she had taken such pains earned hearty commendation from Mr. Fortune.

"There's naught to beat good fresh victuals cooked plain, without a lot of fancy kickshaws and French fol-de-rols," he told the company.

"And a glass of brandy to aid the digestion?" suggested Patrick, waving an inviting hand towards the parlour.

"A very good notion," accepted Mr. Fortune affably. "There's one or two matters I've a mind to talk over with you, and no time like the present, for I should be on my way tomorrow."

Good manners enabled Patrick to conceal his pleasure at this information. Not only did he find his guest exhausting, however well-intentioned, but he was burningly anxious to set things right with Ann, and that meant that he must have her to himself for a little while—a difficult thing to achieve at any time in that busy household and quite impossible while he was encumbered with his duties as host.

He established Mr. Fortune comfortably beside the parlour fire and poured brandy for both of them, wondering what scheme was to be laid before him. Probably some suggestion for improving his starveling acres which would require capital that he had no hope of raising. He settled himself to listen with courteous patience, sipped his brandy and was thus startled into a choking fit when his vis-a-vis said bluntly, "It's about the girl."

By the time that he had recovered his breath, Mr. Fortune was in full flow, and though Patrick had missed the opening phrases there could be no misunderstanding the gist of the gentleman's remarks. "and though I'm not suggesting for a moment that she's not just as safe under your roof as she would be under mine, it won't do. People'll talk. And all the more because you live in this damned remote hole."

"Are you not a little late in reaching this conclusion?" asked Patrick quietly.

Mr. Fortune scratched his chin. "Aye. You have me there, lad," he admitted. "I should have had her out of it months ago. Truth is I was deeply involved just then in a very tricky bit of business. Business that might interest *you*, but we'll talk of that another time. Add to that the fact that she's an independent piece and that I've no legal hold over her, and you'll see my difficulty."

Patrick nodded, not unsympathetically. "And how do you propose to persuade her to your way of thinking? For I am happy to tell you that she finds her work congenial and shows no inclination to desert her post. As you have probably seen for yourself."

Mr. Fortune hesitated for a moment, eyeing his host's hard-bitten countenance doubtfully, and then, characteristically, plunged on.

"Aye. I've seen it. And I've seen more than that."

He paused hopefully. But though Patrick's mouth

188

tightened ominously he only raised an eyebrow in mild enquiry. A little put out by this unco-operative attitude, Mr. Fortune decided to waste no more time on preliminaries.

"Don't tell me you're not tail over top in love with her, for I'd not believe you, me having seen the way you look at her when you think no one's watching. And if she's not nutty on you, then she's only fit for Bedlam. What else d'you think has kept a lass of her quality in thrall to a poverty stricken hill farmer these six months past?"

Plain speaking with a vengeance, thought the slightly dazed Patrick. He could not protest over his own share in the indictment, but the idea that Ann might have developed a tendre for him was arrant nonsense. The hurt inflicted by Lavinia Errol's jilting had cut deep and, in his solitary existence, had festered. Patrick could not envisage a 'lass' of Ann's 'quality' finding him attractive.

He strove to speak temperately. After all, Mr. Fortune was, in some sort, Ann's guardian, and had a right to enquire his intentions. And he was guiltily aware that he had behaved badly in allowing her to stay on at the farm once he had realized that he was in love with her. Just as well as Mr. Fortune did he know the damage that tattling tongues could do to a girl's reputation, but he had yielded to the temptation to keep her close and safe, where he could enjoy her warmth and her loveliness and know that though she could never be his, at least she had not given heart and hand to another. He blamed himself entirely, quite forgetting Ann's own reluctance to go. He said quietly, "So far as my own feelings are in question, you are perfectly correct. I would give all I possess for the right to ask for Miss Beverley's hand in marriage.

189

Unfortunately, 'all I possess' is not sufficient to enable me to support a wife in even modest comfort. She is happy here at the moment, yes. She is young and healthy and the life is new to her. She enjoys the novelty and makes light of privations. But I have seen what such a life can do to a woman, even such as are bred up to it from childhood. A life of unremitting toil, premature ageing, ill-health and, all too often, early death. Do you think I would bring that on the girl I love? No, Mr. Fortune, I was wrong to allow her to stay. Use your best persuasions. Perhaps she will agree to go with you when you leave us tomorrow."

Though he had yielded so promptly to his guest's view of the matter, it was rather astonishing to find that gentleman beaming at him with a geniality that seemed a little excessive under the circumstances, but his mood was too grim to allow of more than a faint, bleak surprise. Moreover Mr. Fortune was replenishing the glasses and obviously settling down to discuss the business in further detail, while all that Patrick desired was to put an early end to the interview and seek a decent solitude.

"Well now," Mr. Fortune began, hitching his chair a little nearer and dropping his voice to a confidential note. "Since we're all agreed so far, let's you and me consider a little further. I don't mind telling you that I came up here in two minds. But I'm inclined to like the cut of your jib, so there's one or two things I'd like to put to you before you come to any rash decisions. Only I can see as you're one that will poker up with family pride as soon as I touch on personal matters, so I'll just ask you to hear me out fairly and not go off at half cock before I'm finished."

Patrick wondered vaguely just how much more personal the fellow could get, but, anxious only to make an end, gave the required undertaking and steeled himself to patient endurance.

"Well first of all there's this family feud with your uncle." He saw the suddenly arrested expression on his host's face, and went on, half apologetically, "No, young Ann knows nothing about it, and it's no bread and butter of mine, you'll be saying. But your uncle's my very good friend—in the way of business, of course —and when he found that I planned to visit you, he charged me with this message. The quarrel, he said, and it no more than a trivial thing at worst—just a spat between brothers—was 'twixt him and your father. If your father had not died untimely it should have been healed e'er this. In so far as he was at fault he regrets it. But he has no quarrel with you. Indeed, as a younker, he liked you pretty well. And when all's said and done, you're his heir, choose how. He'd like to heal the breach between you, have you spend a part of each year at Encliffe. Since the place must come to you some day, you'd best know something of the running of it."

There was a long silence. Then Patrick said gravely, "I have no quarrel with my uncle, nor do I know the rights and wrongs of the dispute. My father was never an easy man. I would be happy to see a foolish feud buried. But I do not count myself my uncle's heir. He is not so far gone in years that he might not yet sire an heir of his body."

It was Mr. Fortune's turn to gape and choke. Surely the young man realized that it took two to make that kind of bargain?

Patrick took pity on him. "I might reasonably have expected to inherit my father's estate," he pointed out. "I would be foolish indeed to count upon succeeding to my uncle's dignities. Moreover I have an odd fancy for

191

making my own way in life, and waiting about for dead men's shoes is *not* my notion of enjoyment."

"Quite so. And very creditable. But you'll allow that your present occupation offers small promise of profit. And, as you yourself admitted, none at all of marriage."

"We will leave my marriage out of this discussion, if you please," interjected Patrick coldly.

Mr. Fortune shrugged. "As you wish. And I suppose next you'll say that you're not interested in making your fortune, since you are already possessed of a large holding in railway stock which, unless I miss my guess, will eventually make you a wealthy man without any effort on your part."

"You appear to be remarkably well acquainted with my affairs," said Patrick, keeping a tight hold on his rising anger. "Was my uncle your informant?"

Mr. Fortune had the grace to look slightly ashamed. "He was. But only because both he and I are involved in the development of those same railways. And let me tell you, young man, that though it may be pockets to let with you at the moment, you may yet live to be thankful for your Papa's far-sightedness."

There could be two opinions about *that*, thought Patrick wearily, and thought it was a reasonable explanation, it did nothing to soothe his growing resentment at what he felt to be an intolerable intrusion upon his private life.

His mood was in no-wise softened when Mr. Fortune added reflectively, "Married Esther Donnington, too, for his second, didn't he? And *she* fell heir to her father's railway holdings if I remember aright."

"Your memory is excellent, sir. Though how all this concerns you I cannot imagine. However, if it will satisfy your curiosity, my father married Miss Donnington with my mother not six months in her grave. I myself never met the unfortunate lady, who died at Philip's birth, but I make no doubt that your insinuations are fully justified. For your further information, his mother's dowry—these all-important railway holdings—will go to Philip when he comes of age. Pray do not hesitate to ask if there are any further details of my family history that are of interest to you."

But irony was wasted on Mr. Fortune. He merely shook his head reproachfully and adjured his host not to be in such a hurry to show hackle. "I'm a plain man and I don't believe in wrapping things up in a lot of fancy words to make em sound better. Which is why I asked you at the outset to give me a fair hearing," he reminded. And Patrick, who thought that he had already shown commendable self-restraint, sighed, and waited for him to continue.

The interruption, however, seemed to have thrown him out of his stride. He sat sipping his brandy thoughtfully for several minutes before he again launched himself into speech, and when he did so his voice lacked something of its former assurance.

"When I set out to come to this wedding, my first notion was to take Ann straight back with me. I'm not saying she'd have come willingly, but there's ways and means of managing that young woman when you know how. I'd only to make out I needed her badly enough and she'd have thought it to be her duty. Well, what with meeting your uncle—which I didn't know till then that he *was* your uncle—and hearing about how you was placed, and then with one or two hints young Barbara let fall, I decided I'd come along and take a look at you myself. Which, barring your trick of pokering up when an older man offers you good advice, and your pig-headed obstinacy in refusing a helping hand from your own flesh and blood, I'll admit I'm not ill-pleased."

For a moment amusement ousted annoyance. Patrick grinned and bowed mock acknowledgement.

Mr. Fortune ignored this irrelevant impudence and pressed on. "I'm to be wed again in two months time," he confided. "I'd reckoned on Ann being happy enough helping Amelia to buy her fal-lals and furbishing up the town house, and then, when we went on honeymoon, I'd thought to place her with some lady of fashion that would take her about a bit in Society. Lady Broughton says such arrangements are quite commonplace and perfectly respectable. Give her the chance to meet some eligible gentleman of her own sort. Never pretended to gentility myself, but the Beverleys may hold up their heads with the best."

He looked up enquiringly, but there was no response. To all appearances Patrick was lending only a polite ear to his remarks. Exasperated, he plunged on, "What's more, she's not a bad looking girl when she's dressed right. You should have seen her at her sister's wedding. Your uncle was quite taken with her. And you yourself will admit that she's a good housekeeper. Once it gets about that she's well-dowered too, she'll have no difficulty in finding a husband."

He waited, hopefully. Patrick said civilly, "An excellent scheme, sir. As you say, the lady will have no difficulty in finding a husband under such circumstances. The trouble is more likely to arise in fending off unwanted suitors."

"And that's the rub," retorted Mr. Fortune smartly. "If she's already set her heart on some other man, I'd just be wasting both time and money, wouldn't I? For she's an obstinate piece as I daresay you've discovered, and once her heart is given she'll never change. Now you don't seem to care over much about money, but let me remind you that *time* lost is gone for ever. If I'd married my Amelia thirty years ago as I wished to do, I'd maybe have had grandchildren of my own by now, and not be fretting myself to flinders over one headstrong chit. So just you take a lesson from me, young man, and don't go wasting the best years of your life!"

"But surely it is Miss Beverley's future that we are considering," suggested Patrick, clutching at the last shreds of his self control. "I am scarcely qualified to give advice, but if I stood in your shoes I should waste no time in putting your excellent scheme into effect."

He rose. It was shockingly ill-bred to indicate so plainly that he had had enough, but it was the simple truth. If the fellow kept on, tempting him almost beyond endurance, so reasonable, so plausible, he could not be answerable for his behaviour.

The hint was taken. Mr. Fortune, apparently conceding defeat, allowed himself to be conducted to his bedchamber. But as Patrick bade him goodnight he seemed to decide on one last throw. "Well—if you must choke yourself on your own pride, you must. But I promised Mary I'd do my best for her girls, and it's a promise I'll keep, for all your looking murder-ripe. Twenty thousand pounds I settled on Barbara and mean to do as much for Ann. With more to follow when I pop off the hooks. So just you think *that* over. And now I'll bid you goodnight and you can take yourself off."

EIGHTEEN

"I'll hap the fire, Janet. And I'll be away early in the morning. Goodnight, my dear. Don't look so sorrowful. We'll come about again, I promise you." Patrick hugged the bowed shoulders and dropped a light kiss on the wrinkled cheek. Janet was a darling, but the need for solitude was paramount. Nor could four walls contain his frustration, the fierce craving for the girl he loved, the urge to snatch at offered happiness regardless of pride and principle.

He walked down to the pool where he had first faced up to the knowledge of his love for Ann Beverley, and alone in the darkness fought out his battle with temptation.

He could not do it. Mr. Fortune, well-meaning but insensitive, could not understand his scruples. And it was small comfort to know that it was scruples—principles—call them what you would, that had laid the snare in which he was now held fast. He had held aloof, done everything in his power to hide his love. What, now, must Ann's feelings be, if, as soon as he was informed that she was an heiress, he proposed marriage? Any girl with an ounce of spirit would send him to the rightabout in no uncertain fashion. Who could believe in a disinterested love under such circumstances? Temptation suggested that there might be something in what Mr. Fortune had said about those railway holdings paying off handsomely. Why not declare his love and ask her to wait for him? The fellow had sounded devilish convincing. But even if he was right, it must surely be several years before one could hope to reap that promised golden harvest. It would be unfair to ask a girl to wait so long while the years of her youth slipped away. A girl, moreover, who now had the opportunity to move in society where she might meet a far more eligible partner.

In the end there was only one decent and honourable course left to him. He must let her go. And freely—unshackled by any hint of his own love, his own desolation. Perhaps she would not be sorry. He would not lightly forget the quivering hurt in her face when he had spoken so unkindly, nor had he missed today's sober looks, the gaiety quenched, the laughter fled. He had meant to beg her forgiveness, but with Mr. Fortune forever on his heels there had been no opportunity, and now it would be better not. Let her go in her present disillusionment. It would ease the parting. And since he must ride into Dent early to arrange for the gig to be sent for the travellers, he could probably avoid anything in the nature of a private farewell. He went back to the parlour to write a short note for Mr. Fortune.

That gentleman counted early rising among his virtues and, the day being fair, went out for a before-breakfast stroll and met Ann on her way back from the poultry yard. He lost no time in acquainting her with the contents of Patrick's note and a truthful, if carefully edited, account of the previous night's conversation.

It was enough. No further persuasion was needed to win her consent to leave with him that day. She even shared Patrick's hope that there would be no opportunity for prolonged leave-taking. As it was the lamentations of the twins were painful enough. Philip, who had been grooming Jigs, came late to breakfast and was promptly informed of the impending blow. He refused to believe until Ann herself confirmed it. Then great tears began to slide down his cheeks and he flung himself at her, clutching desperately, burrowing his hard little head into her breast and sobbing out his sorrow for yesterday's naughtiness with hiccuppy promises of impossible virtue in the future. Ann hugged him close and tried to calm him, assuring him that it was not his fault, that she wasn't a bit cross and loved him dearly. But since she could not add a promise that she would stay after all, his sobs only grew louder. Finally Janet took him from her, suggesting that she had better start on her preparations, with a significant jerk of her head to indicate packing, and rocked him on her lap until he sobbed himself out.

Then she talked to him, quietly and sensibly, reminding him that winter was coming with frost and snow, much too cold for a young lady like Miss Beverley, from which she led gently to the delights of winter as seen by a small boy, and eventually had him quieted, and, she hoped, resigned. He clambered down, with a pathetic resumption of the manhood proper to his seven years, looked with revulsion at his neglected breakfast, and muttered huskily that he was going to talk to

Jigs. Janet let him go. She could do no more for him. He must learn acceptance in his own way.

Ann spent a miserable morning, finishing her packing as quickly as possible only to find that Meg had all the preparations for dinner well in hand. Robert Alder had ridden in just after breakfast having met Patrick and heard that they were still short-handed, and Meg was eager to show how well she could manage on her own. Philip had vanished, and Papa Fortune was sitting glumly in the parlour glancing at a week-old copy of the Intelligencer. He showed no desire for her company and was obviously sadly put out by the failure of his mission. She was reduced to wandering about the place bidding a sorrowful goodbye to objects grown familiar and dear until Janet took pity on her forlorn appearance and asked her to help polish the silver. She was thankful to have her hands occupied, to feel Janet's affection reaching out to her, though the old woman did not talk much. At any other time she would have been full of eager questions about the silver, a rather motley collection which Janet had produced from some hiding place, but today she rubbed mechanically at tarnished spoons and a baby's porringer and did not even question the origin of the crest which adorned a handsome epergne. Janet, watching her beneath lowered lids, made no comment.

"And a waste of time *that* is," was all she said, packing each item carefully away again when they had done. "Never used these days, nor like to be."

Ann, apathetically watching the gnarled hands as they tucked a baby's rattle into one corner of the box, noticed that the handle of this toy could be detached to form a whistle. She thrust a hand into her pocket and said sharply, "Oh dear! I forgot Philip's whistle. I must give it back to him. Have you seen him since breakfast?"

"He went off to the stable to tell his troubles to Jigs, but it's close on dinner time so he'll be coming in."

Ann nodded. "I'll go and fetch him," she said.

But the stable was empty, save for Donna, who turned a friendly head and had to be suitably acknowledged. Going back to the house she felt vaguely uneasy. There was no sign of child or pony in their own fields, and Philip was not supposed to venture further without permission. Besides, it was growing late and the child had eaten no breakfast. Surely hunger should have brought him home by now?

Throughout the meal she was listening for the sound of the pony's hooves, her answers to such remarks as were addressed to her, brief and abstracted, until a happy suggestion from Robert that the little boy had ridden out to meet his brother allayed her anxiety. But when dinner was done, and Meg's beef pudding duly praised, there was still no sign of the absentees. High Garth was so situated that it commanded a view of the north-bound lane for over two miles, but no horseman showed on all that winding track. Ann could not know that Patrick, lingering deliberately in Dent to avoid the possiblity of a tête-á-tête, had then been further detained by the arrival of a messenger from Will, and her anxiety grew with every dragging minute until action of some kind became imperative. She shrank from the notion of riding out to meet Patrick, however valid her reason, but there *was* the possibility that Philip, in sullen defiance of the authority that this morning had so lamentably failed him, had ridden over into Kingsdale. In that case it was possible that some accident had befallen him. And at least, from the head of the dale, she could command a wider view.

Robert was perfectly willing to lend her Donna, and though Mr. Fortune thought she was making a fuss about nothing, Janet admitted that she, for one, would be relieved if that dangerous area could be ruled out of account. She further promised the runaway a hearty spanking when he *did* return, for putting them all to so much trouble and worry. Mr. Fortune heartily agreed to this, but could not see that it was any business of Ann's to go seeking the child.

Ann said quietly, "The charge of Philip is very much my business. It was to ensure his safety as much as to further his education that Mr. Delvercourt employed me; and warned me most particularly of the dangers of letting him wander off alone." She saw the protest in Mr. Fortune's face and went on firmly, "Until I leave the shelter of his roof, I cannot hold myself absolved of that responsibility."

She would not wait to change into riding dress. It was packed at the bottom of her trunk and would take too long. If Philip had been thrown, enough time had been wasted already. And there would be no one in that bleak, savage valley to be shocked by kilted skirts and a display of ankle. Donna was fresh, enjoying the sympathy of the light hands on the rein, and made nothing of the first steep climb. Ann gazed about her eagerly but only steadily browsing sheep and one or two rather scrawny looking cows were to be seen. It was not until she had crossed White Shaw Moss that, with a leap of the heart, she noticed a pony tethered to a tree about half a mile away. She could not see it very clearly because of the tree, but it was about the size and colour of Jigs. She urged Donna to greater effort.

Jigs it was. A forlorn and drooping Jigs who seemed very grateful for their arrival. Of Philip there was no sign. But there was only one place where he could be. Unless he had walked on to one of the farms—and why should he do that, since Jigs was not injured in any way—he must be in one of the caves. There were several in this area, and some of them extremely dangerous. If Philip had met with an accident underground—She shivered, and felt slightly sick.

She called his name, her voice sounding thin and futile, blown away by the wind. There was no answer. No help for it, then. She must master her fear of the subterranean world and go after him.

It seemed reasonable to suppose that he had tethered Jigs as close as possible to his chosen goal, since there were plenty of other small scrubby trees that would have served just as well, so she would explore the nearest cave first. Her knowledge of the caves and their entrances was only from hearsay. She had never actually ventured into them. But the entrance to this one was plain to be seen.

It was not so bad as she had feared. Once her eyes grew accustomed to the dim light she could see that it was a huge place. Cold and dank, but not oppressive. She called again, her voice echoing oddly in the enclosed space. But though she listened intently there was no reply. Somewhere she could hear the sound of running water. Cautiously—for the floor of the cave was anything but smooth—she edged her way forward, calling Philip's name from time to time but without evoking any response. Was he in the cave at all? Perhaps he was just playing a trick on her—a punishment for what he felt was her betrayal—and would come home when hunger and the darkening brought him. He might be hiding somewhere outside—might even have watched her own timorous approach to the entrance. But somehow she felt that he was here. He would never have deserted Jigs. Something was wrong.

She shook herself impatiently. No use becoming fanciful. Near the back of the cave it was so dark that she had to feel the way ahead with outspread hands. She wondered if Philip had planned his escapade far enough ahead to bring a lantern. The water noises were growing louder. Her outstretched hands struck rock, smooth and wet. She had reached the back of the cave. She stopped, perforce, and looked back. The sunlight at the entrance beckoned enticingly. And Philip was not here.

But where was the water that she could hear so plainly? There must be some other outlet to the cave, some crevice or passage that she had missed. She stood perfectly still for a moment, trying to subdue even the sound of her own breathing as she listened, trying to decide the exact direction of the water noises. Then she began to feel her way along the rocky wall to her right. She moved cautiously, a few inches at a time, for it was very dark and at this point the floor of the cave was littered with shale and small boulders, and presently she found what she was seeking. There was an opening in the rock, perhaps three feet high, a little more than three feet wide, and here the clamour of the water was deafening. She guessed at a sizeable waterfall not far away. On hands and knees she crawled forward a yard or two. Useless to call here. The thunder of the tumbling water would drown any lesser sound. And surely, surely not even a venturesome small boy would have crawled into so awesome and constricted a place.

Even on the thought, her outstretched hand touched something soft. It was a child's woollen cap. Not even the almost palpable blackness of the passage could prevent instant identification. Her own hands had stitched the jaunty pheasant's feathers into place, her own work-box furnished the gilded clasp that held them secure. There was no room for further doubt. Philip had gone this way before her and somehow she must find the courage to follow him along that hideous passage.

She never knew how she did it. Certainly she prayed, if not very coherently. As the passage narrowed and the roof seemed to press down on her with all the weight of the hillside above it she found herself muttering scraps of psalms through gritted teeth. She clutched Philip's cap as though it was some precious talisman. And she went on. She dragged her terrified, shivering body over the wet shale, sometimes on hands and knees, sometimes crawling, so low was the roof, her senses numbed by the roar of the waterfall so that she scarcely felt hands rubbed raw by the rough shale or the pain from sundry cuts and bruises.

The passage seemed to go on for ever. She felt that she had been struggling through nightmare for hours. But presently, through her terror and her desperate determination she became aware of some change. She rested for a moment, trying to identify the difference, and realized that she had left the thunder of the waterfall behind. Probably this passage was some sort of drain, an overflow from the main stream. Wearily now, she set off again, scarcely realizing that the passage was widening until she reached a place where she could no longer touch both walls. The left hand one had vanished, and the rock beneath her hand, though smooth and water-worn, was dry.

She hauled herself out of the stream bed and lay breathless for a moment, wondering how much longer this macabre game of hide and seek was destined to last—and heard the sobbing of a child. For a moment she thought she had imagined it. She said fearfully, hopefully, "Philip?"

The sobbing stopped. He made an odd little whimpering sound, heart-breaking in its mixture of despair and tremulous hope.

She said quickly, clearly, "Philip! I can't see you, but I can hear you. Stay where you are, and *I'll* come to *you*. Could you make a noise—clap your hands perhaps—to guide me?"

She waited, straining her ears, and after an anxious moment while a terrified little boy tried to grasp what was required of him, heard a feeble patter that was sweeter than music in her ears. Fatigue, and the dangers that yet might lie ahead were all forgotten as she crawled towards the sound. He was not very far away, huddled in a soaking, shivering heap, too numb with cold and fear to do more than flop against her as her eager searching hands found him. She pulled him into her arms and hugged him close. He was shaking with cold and she tried to rub his limbs to get some warmth back into him. And as she rubbed she talked, inconsequent cheerful chatter that might, she hoped, lessen the impact of his shocking experience and make his world seem normal again. It appeared to be a losing battle. He did not answer, indeed showed no sign of vitality at all save for his desperate clutch on the front of her dress. Then a happy reference to Jigs and a mention of leaving Donna to keep him company, turned the trick. A husky little voice asked if the pony was all right and upon being assured that he was quite all right but had seemed very pleased to see them, a much more Philip-like voice announced, "So was I very pleased to see you. Except I *can't* see you."

Once having turned the corner his recovery was steady. But he was still very cold, and Ann knew that hot drinks and a warm bed were urgently needed if he was not to take a serious chill. She had no idea how long he had been in the cavern and he was in no state to be questioned. Instead she told him how frightened *she* had been in the darkness of the passage and how much braver she would feel going back now that there were two of them. Privately she was desperately anxious as to her ability to negotiate the passage at all, encumbered by a dazed and weakened child. But the attempt must be made. Already the warmth created by her exertions was dying, the deadly, insidious chill of the place seeping into her bones. And intense cold, she had read somewhere, dulled the mind, caused one to abandon the effort to survive and to yield to a languor that could swiftly prove fatal. They had better start soon.

Philip said slowly, "But we can't go back. Not without a lantern. And I d-dropped it and it went out." And at long last the tears came and he sobbed bitterly in her arms.

She fondled him like a baby, crooning nonsense words, rubbing her cheek against his soft hair until eventually he quieted. The tears had done him good, she thought, for now he snuggled contentedly into her hold and even put up a tentative hand to feel for her face, while his words, when they did come, were a sensible explanation of their position.

"We must wait till Patrick comes for us. There are lots of passages, and in the dark you could make a mistake. Some of them are very dangerous. Patrick said, 'If ever you are lost, sit still and wait till I come for you.' So I did. But it was such a *long* time, and I was so cold and hungry. And then it was only you."

Chilled and anxious as she was, Ann chuckled. One didn't expect polished courtesy from small boys, but really! Even Philip seemed to feel that something was amiss, for he added in extenuation, "You see he knows the passages and you don't."

"But of course," agreed Ann, smiling to herself in the darkness. "And they're bound to find us pretty soon, because of Jigs and Donna. So all we have to do is keep as warm as we can till the rescue party arrives!"

Nevertheless it seemed a very long time before that blessed glimpse of light wavered towards them from the mouth of the passage. They had clapped and stamped and waved their arms like windmills. They had played guessing games and sung all the nursery rhymes that they knew. Ann had discovered Philip's whistle still in her pocket, and from time to time he blew on it to indicate their whereabouts to the rescue party. She was racking her brain for further ways of distracting his mind from his increasing miseries when his shriek of delight informed her that help had arrived.

There were two lanterns bobbing towards them. Robert was only a yard or two behind Patrick. Philip struggled up and hobbled stiffly towards his brother, to be scooped up in one arm. But Patrick's other hand lifted the lantern so that its light could sweep the shelf on which the two had been huddled. There was a sharp exclamation. He put down the lantern, turned and handed the child to Robert and strode towards Ann, catching her in his arms and kissing her with a savage intensity that sprang more from his great fear for her and its relief than from his adoring love.

"Ann! My darling!" he said hoarsely. "Thank God! If harm had come to you"—and he shuddered and gulped convulsively as he thought of the hideous death that she had escaped, it seemed, by divine providence. There, in the flickering lantern light, under the gaze of an admiring Robert and a slightly shocked Philip, he proceeded to kiss her again. Very comprehensively, but so gently, so lightly, lips scarcely brushing her brow, her cheek, her mouth, that his actions seemed more in the nature of a heartfelt thanksgiving than of lovemaking. It was not until Ann, who found this treatment remarkably effective in overcoming fatigue and shock, put her arms round his neck and returned his kisses with what could only be described as enthusiasm, that he seemed to realize what he was doing. He put her from him with an odd shaken little laugh, and still keeping one arm about her as though he could not bear to let her go.

"Forgive me," he said quietly. "It was the thankfulness, you see. We could not be sure you were together. And when I heard the whistle and saw only Philip, I feared for a moment"—and his arm tightened about her as though he was still not wholly sure of her reality.

Ann turned her cheek into his shoulder and snuggled into it with perfect confidence. "Pray don't apologize," she said, on an irrepressible bubble of laughter. "I enjoyed it of all things. But I *could* think of more suitable surroundings in which to—er—pursue the matter further."

A snort of amusement from Robert at this sally served to bring Patrick to his senses. "Yes, indeed," he agreed cheerfully. "The sooner we're out of this grisly hole, the better. Will you go first, Robert? Then Philip. One more big effort, brat. You can do it, I know. Keep close to Robert and he'll look after you. Our turn next, sweetheart. We'll soon have you safe."

Ann was a little startled to see Robert wriggle himself *backwards* into the passage, but Patrick explained that in this way he could help the child better, taking his hands or his shoulders to ease him over the roughest places. "We shall use the same method. But first"—He stripped off his jacket and buttoned her into it despite her protests. "Do as you're told," he said calmly. "It will save a few grazes —and you need the extra warmth."

"Not now," she murmured demurely, an audacity that was acknowledged by a swift, hard kiss. Then, as Philip's feet vanished from sight, he gave her an encouraging grin and backed into the passage.

Despite his cheerful promise it was a slow and awkward business. But it was surprising how much difference it made to have the rather wayward illumination of the lanterns, and, far more vital, the firm clasp of Patrick's hand on hers. She even found time and breath to tell him so—only about the *lanterns*, of course—as they waited for the pair ahead to negotiate a tricky turn.

"You came this way without a lamp?" And before she could answer, "But of course, you must have done. I had not thought"—and then, very softly, "And I almost let you go. Through stupid pride."

It was a shock to emerge into the main cavern to find that it was still daylight. Patrick lifted her, now, and carried her out into the blessed sunlight, ignoring assurances that she could perfectly well walk, and set her on her feet beside the horses. Robert was rolling a disgusted Philip into a blanket cocoon. "Like a baby," protested that young gentleman.

"And no more sense than one," retorted Robert. "Just you bide quiet. You've given us trouble enough for one day." And then, relenting at the sight of a

209

trembling lip, "Though you showed good sense blowing that whistle." He lifted the little boy on to Jigs's back and set off at a gentle amble, leading the pony with one hand and holding Philip safely in the saddle with the other.

One horrified glance at her own appearance and Ann was only too thankful to accept her own enshrouding blanket. Her dress was in rags, her hair had come down and her plaits were liberally bedaubed with mud, while bare pink toes were peeping through the wreck of one shoe. Not at all the image that a young lady would choose to present to a newly declared lover. Any lingering doubts that she might have entertained on that score were removed as he wrapped the blanket round her. He had resumed his own jacket, to reveal the sleeve of her gown ripped from shoulder to elbow and a purplish weal, the blood already dried on it, disfiguring the soft curve of her arm. A swift little murmur of pity escaped him and he set gentle lips to the bruise.

"More honourable scars for a Beverley," he said slowly. And then, "Will you change your name for mine, beloved? For indeed I cannot bear to let you go."

The glow in the big brown eyes was answer enough. She said steadily, "To be your wife is the greatest good that I could desire. I shall be proud and happy to take your name and to share your life. Why *should* you let me go, when all I want is to be with you always?"

His lips twisted ruefully as he tucked the blanket firmly round her. "I'm not much of a match, you know. You could do a good deal better for yourself. I had meant to let your step-papa have his way and present you in Society, but I find I cannot do without you after all."

"Oh, I daresay Papa Fortune will raise every kind of objection," said Ann cheerfully. "He was talking of this scheme for firing me off, only this morning, but I'm afraid I wasn't paying much attention. In any case I'm of age, so he can't forbid the banns."

Patrick hid his surprise. It had seemed to him that Papa Fortune was only too anxious to hear the publication of those particular banns. But it would sound shockingly conceited to say so. Besides, it was more important at the moment to get his promised bride to warmth and shelter, where her hurts could be properly looked to.

"Can you manage to cling to the pommel if I lead Donna?" he enquired, lifting her into the saddle and looking up at her lovingly, bruises, mud and all. And the independent Miss Beverley meekly admitted that her hands *were* very sore, and that she was thankful that she was not obliged to control even the gentle Donna.

NINETEEN

"I gathered that she knew nothing of the financial settlement that you proposed," said Patrick.

Mr. Fortune regarded him with indulgent pity. "What! Tell a woman anything about money matters? It's more than most of them can do to balance their household books. Of course she doesn't know. It's you and me that must put on our thinking caps and decide what's best to be done. I know of one or two nice little businesses that could use a bit more capital. It's just a question of choosing the right one and buying an interest, and though I say it myself there's nobody can advise you better than me." And he began to enumerate the various snug little enterprises that would richly repay the investment of money and energy, until a knock on the parlour door heralded the arrival of Meg with a supper tray.

As soon as the rescue party had reached the farm, Janet had taken charge, banishing the menfolk from the kitchen. Philip was swiftly dealt with, by the simple process of popping him into a washtub in front of the fire. By the time that he had been dried off and had devoured a basin of bread and milk he was already nodding, and his objections to being put to bed so early trailed off into a huge yawn.

While Janet and Jenny attended to Ann, Meg served the gentlemen in the parlour with a hastily assembled meal, apologizing that she could only offer them pickled beef with apple pie and cheese to follow as there had been no time to dress a proper supper.

Meg was very happy. Robert had gone home, rather reluctantly, before the darkening, but he was sure that his father could spare him again tomorrow. It was clear—to Robert and Meg, at any rate—that High Garth stood in great need of neighbourly support. Apart from their natural delight in being together, not for worlds would Robert have missed the unfolding of the drama in which he had played so useful a part. He was consumed with curiosity as to its outcome. Meg thought it was very probable that he would arrive in time to help with the morning milking.

Mr. Fortune, too, was in his most expansive mood. The irritability consequent upon the inevitable delay in his journey—and all on account of a headstrong girl's foolish cantrips—had vanished like magic when Patrick, doing the thing in style, formally requested his consent to the marriage. He had given it with enthusiasm. Not knowing the countryside, not understanding the appalling risk that Ann had taken, he was inclined to ascribe this happy issue to his own persuasive abilities and to Patrick's good sense. At any other time Patrick might have found his slightly smug delight infuriating. But he, too, was in happy mood. His beloved girl had consented to marry him, not for the problematical wealth and rank that he might some day be able to bestow upon her, but because she loved him and wanted to spend the rest of her life with him. In such a case he could afford to ignore a few minor rubs.

So Mr. Fortune spent a very pleasant evening working out wedding plans and future domestic arrangements for the young couple, while Patrick, apart from a few moments spent in wondering in just what relationship he would stand to this benevolent despot when he and Ann were wed, allowed them all to flow over him and gave himself up to his own reflections.

Neither gentleman was permitted another glimpse of the heroine of the occasion. Upon enquiry they were told that Janet had persuaded 'the young mistress' to swallow a few drops of syrup of poppies, and that she was now tucked up in bed with a hot brick to her feet. Mr. Fortune commended this treatment. Not that he was, in general, an advocate of young folks quacking themselves, but it would not do to have the girl taking cold just now, with so much to be set in hand.

Patrick, cocking an amused eyebrow at Janet, wondered just how long Ann had been 'the young mistress'. He had not thought it proper to take his old nurse into his confidence before he had approached Mr. Fortune, and he considered it unlikely that Ann had done so. It seemed that Bridie was not the only one who could foretell the future!

The thought of Bridie recalled to mind certain problems with which he had been much preoccupied until the news that Philip and Ann were missing had driven every other thought from his head. Having seen Mr. Fortune safely bestowed for the night, he returned to the kitchen to consult with Janet.

"I had news of Will and Bridie while I was in Dent,"

214

he began. "Will had sent a message with the carrier, wanting to know if he can bring Bridie to us when she can be moved, which will be any day now. And thinking that we would have room and to spare, I sent back word to come as soon as they liked. To speak truth, I doubt if Bridie'll be fit for the road again before spring. If then. She might settle here—with Will."

Janet pursed her lips. "We'll be a bit pushed," she said thoughtfully, "till the gentleman goes. Philip had best move in with me and Bridie can have his room. Is Miss Ann staying on after all?" she added, innocent-faced, unaware of her earlier slip of the tongue.

Patrick hugged her. "That seems to be the general idea," he told her solemnly, eyes full of laughter. "You see Philip can't do without her."

"Oh! So it's *Philip* that can't do without her is it? I've a notion he's not the only one," retorted Janet tartly.

"No. But he went to considerable lengths to prove his point, didn't he?"

Janet sobered. "Aye. That was a fearsome thing Miss Ann did. I'd not have ventured in there alone and without a light for a thousand pounds—and her afraid of caves from a child, she was telling me."

"We'll need to take better care of her in the future," agreed Patrick gravely. "What's more there is a little matter of disobedience to be dealt with. Both of them had been straitly forbidden to leave the valley. But they were in no case for scolding."

"I should think not, indeed," said Janet indignantly. "Better you went down on your knees to thank God."

"Do you think I didn't? And will for the rest of my life. But there is no excuse for Philip's disobedience. And to put another life in danger—"

"Well, you can't blame the child for *that*," said

215

Janet fairly. "Once he was *in* trouble, he did exactly as you told him. 'Twasn't *his* fault that Miss Ann went in after him. And from what she says it was thanks to him that she didn't try to make her way back. So don't be too hard on him."

Patrick was in no mood to be hard on anyone. Nor did he believe in keeping retribution hanging over a sinner's head for ever. Justice should be prompt, especially where a child was concerned, and Philip's subdued mien at breakfast next day would have touched a harder heart than his brother's.

It was an unusually late and leisurely breakfast for a farmhouse, and except for Jim, busy with the sheep salving, they were all gathered round the big table together. Robert, enjoying a second breakfast, looked from face to face and tried to catch Philip's eye to give him an encouraging wink, but Philip's gaze was bent on his plate, and despite the cream that Janet had surreptitiously poured on his porridge he was making slow progress.

Kindest to put the poor little devil out of his misery, thought Patrick. "Well, young Philip," he said briskly, "and what took you into Kingsdale yesterday? Against orders, too. And into the Gullet, of all places."

Philip's spoon went down with a clatter and the childish chin quivered, but he held his head up and met his brother's eyes bravely enough.

"I knew if I asked you, you wouldn't let me go," he admitted in a rather wobbly voice. And then, the worst over, went on more confidently, "And I wanted to find the gold. I thought if we could find it, we could all go back to the Court to live and then Miss Beverley needn't leave us. Janet said it was too cold for her to stay here in winter when the snow comes, but she'd be nice and warm at the Court, wouldn't she?"

There was a gasp from Janet, and a sound somewhere between a snort and a choke from Mr. Fortune. "Why, you young rapscallion!" he said, almost admiringly. For you couldn't deny that the lad had gone straight to the nub of the matter and shown both business acumen and enterprise. "What gold is this?"

"Oh—some fabulous hoard—Viking or Jewish—reputedly hidden in the caves," Patrick said impatiently. "Probably non-existent, and in any case nobody knows which cave. But what possessed you to go into the Gullet, brat? You knew it was a bad place."

Something in voice and face informed Philip that justice was to be tempered with mercy. He took courage to defend himself.

"That's why," he said simply. "Because it *is* a bad place. If I wanted to hide a treasure, I'd *put* it in a bad place, so that people would be afraid to go and look for it."

There was no mistaking the admiration on Mr. Fortune's face. "Well I call that good sound sense," he said approvingly. Patrick broke in swiftly before discipline was irretrievably wrecked.

"Perhaps you should first understand just how 'bad' a place the Gullet is," he said drily. "There are several connecting passages that lead to it. The Gullet itself is a sink-hole."

Mr. Fortune looked puzzled. The word, in this connection, was new to him.

Patrick said, "There is an underground stream which plunges some forty feet into this funnel shaped hole—the Gullet—and then disappears underground. There is a whirlpool which could drag down the strongest swimmer. After heavy rain the whole system is full of water—and it can fill in half an hour. When

217

that happens there is no hope of escape for anyone caught in the passages."

There was a nasty little silence. Mr. Fortune looked crestfallen, Philip crushed.

Ann said gently, "It was very wrong of us both to disobey orders. I disobeyed too, Philip. But perhaps if we are truly sorry, your brother won't be so very angry with us." She looked up at that brother, a little shy still of her new-found happiness, and added softly, "And after all—we did find the gold, didn't we?"

Patrick's rather harsh features softened almost unbelievably with mingled love and laughter. "Now see what you've done," he chided. "Raised poor Philip's hopes. He thinks we must have stumbled on the hidden treasure. No, Philip, we didn't. We were thankful enough to get out with whole skins. But the lady is in the right of it. We did, in a sense, find gold. Of a kind worth more than any mythical metal. And thanks largely to your intervention, Miss Beverley *is* going to stay with us. For always, because she is going to marry me. And we *are* going back to the Court, though we shall often be at High Garth too, especially in summer."

Among the babel of joyous exclamation and congratulation that broke out at this, the only dissident voice—and the most easily heard—was that of Mr. Fortune.

"But you can't conduct a business from an out-of-the-way place like the Court," he protested, "however fine and comfortable it may be."

"Oh, yes you can, sir!" retorted Patrick cheerfully. "What's more, it's the only business for which I've any aptitude. Farming. Now don't pull a wry mouth. I'll hope to bring you round to my way of thinking when we have the chance of a little rational talk away from this noisy rabble. I've known for some years what I'd like to do if ever the chance came my way. Thanks to you it *has* come, since you insist on making my wife a wealthy woman. You're used to the fat corn lands of the south, sir. But there's good farm land here, too, for all its harsh seeming. Best pasture in England for cheesemaking, because of the herbs that grow on the limestone. Good, too, for horse breeding and breaking. But what I'd chiefly rely upon is trading in cattle. Buying in the Scots beef cattle and fattening 'em up for market. There's a growing demand in the towns for beef and butter and cheese. And when these wonderful railways that we hear so much about are all built, there'll be no trouble about getting our produce to market, will there?" he finished, with a twinkle that drew a reluctant grin from his adversary.

"There's some sense in what you say," that gentleman allowed. "But I doubt your wife won't like it. Buried in the country all the year round when she could be queening it in the parlours and ballrooms."

"Oh! Am I concerned in this?" demanded a suspiciously innocent voice.

"Well—it's your life, isn't it, as well as his?" returned Mr. Fortune bluntly.

Ann considered this carefully. Then she said, "I don't care above half for balls and parlour parties. But I *do* like pretty clothes and going to the play and watching the notables parade in the Park. Perhaps if we get rich in this new kind of farming, we can go up to Town sometimes. And then we can come and visit with you and Mrs. Fortune," she told her step-father kindly. "But if I must choose between Town and country, there can be no question which I prefer. And won't Will love it?" She turned a radiant face on Patrick. "All those cattle to look after! Though I must confess," she added pensively, "that I don't care much for Scots cattle! They have such very sharp looking horns. Must we have that kind?"

Patrick laughed and promised to consult with Will on this vital point. Which reminded him to tell her the news about Will and Bridie.

"Dear Bridie!" said the girl affectionately. "I shall be so happy to see her again. She was so very kind to me." Her thoughts turned to the evening when Bridie had told their fortunes and her eyes widened a little. "So many of the things she told me have come true," she said, striving to recall the details that she had so lightly dismissed. "Why! She even said something about going down into the dark waters. I suppose that means the Gullet—or perhaps being so frightened," she finished thoughtfully. And then her face lit to eagerness and she exclaimed, "Oh! Perhaps she'll be able to tell me how many chil—" And broke off, scarlet with confusion, as her glance fell on the absorbed faces of her audience.

Fortunately her step-papa, who had been champing impatiently over this long digression about people who meant nothing to him, plunged into the breach by demanding loudly when the wedding was to be and where they proposed to be married.

Patrick turned to Ann. "That is for you to say, my love, though I hope you do not mean to keep me waiting too long."

She hesitated. Her cheeks were still burning, her own incautious remark still sounding in her ears. If she said what she longed to say, they would all smile again.

Janet, deeply interested herself, was nevertheless affronted that such lowly members of the household as the twins, not to mention Robert, who wasn't even one of them, should be permitted to witness so intimate a scene. She seized upon Ann's hesitation to say quietly, "Maybe you'd rather discuss that in the parlour, Miss Ann. It's high time we got this kitchen redded up or there'll be no dinner for any of you."

At which point a small voice said, "What about me?"

Philip, forgotten in the general excitement, stood his ground bravely, determined to know the worst. Patrick dropped a hand on his shoulder and said gravely, "*You* will give me your word of honour as a gentleman that you will not again go into the caves without first consulting me."

Philip seemed to add an inch to his stature. "I give you my word," he said clearly, eyes huge with the solemnity of his new dignity.

His brother grinned and tousled his head. "You're forgiven then," he said. "Be off and give Jigs a good currying. And when we go back to the Court, it's school for you, my lad. There's a good one in Dent Town. You can ride in every day."

So much excitement was too much for Philip to contain. He bounded off to tell Jigs all about it.

In the parlour Patrick turned expectantly to Ann. "Well, my darling?"

She smiled at him. "As soon as it can be arranged," she said simply. "St. Andrew's?"

St. Andrew's was the little church in Dent Town. On being apprised of this, Mr. Fortune said explosively, "Well! I should think your uncle will have something to say about *that* His heir to be married in such haste and such a hugger-mugger fashion. If ever I met such a mad-brained pair! Why! I'm sure his lordship would lend his Town house for such an occasion and do the thing in prime style."

221

"Which is just what we don't want," said Patrick smoothly, avoiding Ann's face of bewildered enquiry. "A quiet wedding with all our friends about us. My uncle will be very welcome if he chooses to honour us. And you'll come, won't you, sir, despite your disapproval? And as soon as we're wed, we'll come home to High Garth," he promised Ann.

The indignant Mr. Fortune then announced that he washed his hands of the whole affair and would leave them to make their own plans, and, with unexpected tact, took himself off to the kitchen, where, for lack of any other confidant he poured out his complaints to the sympathetic Janet.

Patrick acted swiftly. Before Ann could utter a syllable he stopped her mouth with kisses. Not until she clung, warm and pliant in his arms, did he draw back a little, and then his remarks were nicely calculated to rob her of any remaining breath.

"You're really rather nice to kiss, now that you've washed the mud off your face," he told her kindly. "You must remind me to try it again some time."

A tiny choke of laughter escaped her, but she made a quick recover. "Thank you, sir. You are much too good," she told him demurely, "but I would not dream of presuming so far. And now, perhaps, you will be so kind as to tell me who *is* this uncle who is so important? Whose heir you are?"

Opportunites for laughter and teasing had been rare enough in Patrick's life. This one was irrestible. "My uncle?" he enquired, in a tone of innocent surprise. "Why—he is my father's brother, you know. His *elder* brother," he elaborated conscientiously. "My mother, too, had only the one brother, the uncle who bequeathed me High Garth, so this one is my only surviving uncle. He and my father were"—

He was rudely interrupted. Two small hands were now twisted in his hair, tugging and shaking unmercifully so that he was forced to sue for peace.

"Very well. Now tell me properly," said the lady sternly.

"But it was all true," protested the sinner plaintively. "He *was* my father's only brother. But because he is the elder, he is the Earl of Encliffe. And because he and his wife are unfortunately childless, I *am* his heir. Which is why Papa Fortune was making such a bother."

She stared at him in some dismay, remembering the gentleman who had singled her out with so much kindness at Barbara's wedding. So that was why he had shown such interest in the affairs of High Garth. And unless the Countess was very much younger than her husband it did, indeed, seem probable that Patrick would in due course succeed to the title.

"But I don't think I want to be a Countess," she said slowly.

"Well, if it comes to that, I didn't want to marry an heiress," said Patrick reasonably. "But it's surprising how quickly one can accustom oneself, once the fatal step is taken. I'll be honest and confess that I'm beginning to like the idea pretty well, now that I'm getting used to it. Just think of all the things we'll be able to do for the Court and for Philip and"—he hugged her joyously—"for all those children you were so indiscreet as to suggest."

She shook her head at him, blushing again, but she laughed. He said, on a suddenly serious note, "That's if you really mean it. If you really prefer the kind of life I'd dreamed of. I find it hard to believe. But then I find *you* hard to believe. That you should have happened to me, I mean." And realizing that he was becoming slightly incoherent, he explained himself in more direct fashion.

When she had breath enough Ann said, "Of course I meant it, goose. You know how I've loved being at High Garth. And being your wife will make it quite perfect. Then I shall feel that I'm really a part of it. Although I fell in love with the Court at first sight, I shall leave a bit of my heart at High Garth."

Well you won't have to leave it just yet," said Patrick cheerfully. "Conroy's lease isn't up till Lady Day. You've still to face a winter here. And despite Janet's gloomy warnings and Philip's fears, I think you'll like it. Plenty to do, plans to be made, and fi we're snowed up—which we frequently are—a little world of our own. Just think of it! No morning callers—no bride visits—heaven!"

"Well it's much more my idea of heaven than being a Countess," admitted his betrothed.

"And I'll have no more complaints on *that* score," announced this newly confident Patrick. "*You* said, bless you, that all you wanted was to share my life. And so you shall. While I am a farmer, you're a farmer's wife. But fi chance makes me an Earl, then it makes you a Countess. I daresay we shall learn to like it well enough with practice. But meanwhile there's our marriage to arrange and then a whole peaceful winter in our private kingdom. And if the time *should* chance to hang heavily on our hands in the long winter evenings," he ended mischievously, "we can always get Bridie to look into the future for us!"